I0460377

Thirty Below

a novel by

Harry Groome

THE
CONNELLY
PRESS

Originally published as an e-book edition by The Connelly Press in February 2012.

HARD HEARTED HANNAH (THE VAMP OF SAVANNAH)
Words and Music by Jack Yellen, Milton Ager, Bob Bigelow and Charles Bates
© 1924 (Renewed) Warner Bros. Inc. (ASCAP) and Edwin H. Morris and Company,
a division of MPL Music Publishing, Inc.
All Rights Reserved
Used by Permission of Alfred Music Publishing Co., Inc.
and the Hal Leonard Corporation

Excerpt from IN THE LAKE OF THE WOODS
by Tim O'Brien (Boston: Houghton Mifflin, 1994)

Cover design: HG for Hire
Cover photograph: Jack Berry

ISBN: 0979741556
ISBN 13: 978-0-9797415-5-5
eISBN: 978-0-9797415-4-8
Library of Congress Control Number 2014931041
The Connelly Press, Villanova, PA

ALSO BY HARRY GROOME

Wing Walking
The Girl Who Fished with a Worm

for my natal pack

"The snows and the camp-fire, with wolves at my feet.
Good-bye, for it's safer up there."
—Robert Service

"One must always arrive with a story to tell after having gone to the wilderness; that's how it is!"
—Traditional Native Alaskan narrative

1

HER ADVENTURE BEGAN on a Saturday, one much like every Saturday in her life, a life she would describe as "going nowhere, unless you consider a dead-end somewhere." Adele Caroline Ritter, called Carrie by almost everyone for as long as she could remember, was standing in her morning shower thinking being warm was the best part of her life. She loved the warm weather in southern California; loved lying around at the beach, loved her tanning salon, and loved taking hot showers at the start of every day. She thought all were warm and good and with all these good warm things at her fingertips, what more could a girl want? The thought caused her to let out a short laugh for the answer was more. Tons more.

The man of her dreams for starters.

And a new job.

And a change of scene.

And anything else that would be new and exciting.

She kneaded shampoo into her blonde curls and, for a moment, wondered about the weather in Alaska and then turned the shower dial past the red temperature-warning button and raised her chin so the water hit the top of her head, rinsed her soapy shoulders and washed over her back and hips and down her legs and swirled around her narrow, long-toed feet. She pressed her hands against the shower wall, inspected her nails and thought she'd get a manicure, something she did every Saturday because it was part of being a professional even though most of the time her hands were hidden in vinyl gloves. She turned her hands front and back. Not ugly, she thought, but big. Really big. It was a wonder one of her patients hadn't said something.

While she was thinking about the size of her hands she thought she heard a sound in the living room and pushed open the shower door and called, "Hannah, that you?" but the small apartment was quiet except for the pulsing hum of the air conditioners. She listened a moment longer and stepped back under the shower and began to sing to feel less alone. She sang *Hard Hearted Hannah*, the song she thought must have been written about her roommate, Hannah Hall. She was singing, "Talk of your cold, refrigerating mammas, brother, she's the polar bear's pajamas!" when once more she thought she'd heard a noise in the living room. Again she pushed the shower door open and leaned her head out. "Hannah? You home?"

Still there was no answer. "Hello!" she said, and waited. "Hello? Is anybody there?"

Maybe Hannah's right, she thought. Maybe she should give up caffeine or maybe tonight's long-awaited date had put her on edge. She took a deep breath and forced herself to relax and watched the water rinse the soapy bubbles from her breasts. Not flat as pancakes, but not great either and she wondered if old Doctor-Boobs-dot-com, or whatever his name was, could help. It wasn't like maxillofacial surgery or anything; it was only a couple of incisions and silicone shells for Pete's sake. Maybe it would be worth the $7,500 if it would help her find Mr. Right.

She turned off the shower and swept water from her thighs and calves. When she finished drying herself, she draped her towel over the sink and stepped on the scales. Her weight hadn't changed since college and it was one of the few constants in her life that pleased her, for she knew from her years of being a swimmer at USC that one hundred and forty-six pounds was the right weight for a woman with her build who stood five feet eleven inches tall. She rewrapped her towel and began to blow dry her hair, adding another mental note to tell her hairdresser that she was tired of her curly blonde ponytail hanging from the back of a baseball cap like all the other girls in La Jolla and that she had to do something new and different.

The idea of something new made her smile, something she felt she should do more often because, by her own professional analysis, her teeth were straight, a good size and a one or a two on the tooth shade whiteness scale. "The perfect pearly whites for a dental hygienist," was the constant refrain of the dentist she worked for, and she shook her head as she swept the blow dryer over her curls, silently cursing her boss for standing too close to her in the examining room, occasionally pressing against her or brushing her butt with his small, delicate hands. She dismissed these thoughts as part of a bigger problem, moved the blow dryer quickly about her head, and decided to take inventory.

She began by focusing on her large green eyes in the mirror, gave them a better than average grade and thought her teeth and weight were okay, maybe even better than okay, but worried that she was too tall for most men and that her hands and feet were too large. Her breasts were adequate, but nothing to write home about. Her hair color also was nothing special, although she thought her tight curls were distinctive—kind of her trademark—and shook her head and said aloud, "But shoulders like a linebacker, and hips like a little boy."

When she'd almost finished drying her hair, for what seemed like the thousandth time, she debated the pros and cons of getting the tattoo that most people never saw. Why did I ever do that, she wondered. For breaking sixty seconds in the 100-meter fly, that's why. She unwrapped her towel and began to turn to look in the mirror at the red and blue tattoo of a butterfly on the small of her tanned back, to re-convince herself that it was stylish—hopefully even sexy—but as she turned, she saw something flicker in the corner of the mirror and held the blow dryer still above her shoulder. Her heart began to race and her body shook with adrenalin when a thick forearm covered with coarse black hair slid across her breasts and pulled her hard against its owner.

Carrie screamed for holy Jesus and looked in the mirror at a tall man pressing against her from behind. She expected to see a stranger wearing a stocking or a ski mask over his head but instead, Jake Hornbeck was undisguised and laughing, his muscular body naked from the waist up.

"Scare you?" he said.

"What do you think?" Carrie said, struggling to pry his arm from her chest. "Now let go of me."

Her efforts only seemed to tighten his grasp and she felt a sudden rush of panic as she realized that she was at this man's mercy for he was the strongest man she'd ever encountered, certainly way too strong for her. "Jake, let go of me," she said again, and told him that he wasn't funny, but as she pleaded with him she felt his arm tighten even more, and watched the muscles of his forearm flex, and for an instant thought that his heavily haired arm looked so out of place pressing against her breasts, still pink from the warm shower. "Please, Jake," she coughed out, "I don't like this and you know it. Remember? The rough stuff is one of the—"

"Ah, come on, Carrie," he interrupted, and continued to grin at her in the mirror. "I thought I'd give you a surprise. To change your mind about Alaska."

"It's not about Alaska, Jake. It's about you and me. And no matter what you do you can't change my mind about us." She stared at him in the mirror, trying to sort through her thoughts that were now jumbled by fear. "How did you get in here anyway?"

"You gave me a key, remember?"

"But that was before..." She turned off the blow dryer and placed it in the sink. Even though she was having a hard time breathing, the bathroom seemed a little more settled, even a bit more hopeful, without the whirring sound. She rested her hands on the sides of the basin and tried to draw a full breath, all the while staring at Jake in the mirror. She was repulsed by the *Death Before Dishonor* and scorpion tattoos on his biceps and shoulder. They said so much about him; reflected his dark side that it had taken her so long to discover.

Jake stared back at her, smiling broadly, something Carrie thought definitely didn't fit the situation. She stood motionless, her hands still resting on the basin and struggled to regain her composure. She waited a moment and then said, as calmly as she could, "Jake, please, be nice and let go of me. We agreed we were through with all this. Why can't we just be friends?"

"Because that's not the way I'm wired." The smile left his face as quickly as it had appeared. "I don't give up that easily; certainly not to some son of a bitch you haven't even met." He bit her earlobe. "One more time, Carrie, to see what you'll be missing," he said, and promised that he'd make it fun, more fun than she'd have in Alaska.

"Jake, listen to me." She slapped her hands on the edges of the basin. "This is not my idea of fun! Besides, Hannah's due home any minute."

"Nice try, big girl, but she's worked Saturdays ever since I've known you."

She said Hannah had the day off.

"I'll take my chances," he said and began to run his free hand back and forth across her belly and then moved his fingers between her legs.

Carrie screamed, "No!" and grabbed for his hand only to find her hand in his grip, and again she thought he had almost superhuman strength. "Jake," she pleaded, "please take me seriously. I'm asking you to take your hands off me and leave. This has gone far enough, so out and out now. Please, before Hannah comes home. Before this goes any further."

The phone rang. "I've got to get that. I'm expecting a call from my mom."

It rang a second time. "She's sick."

Jake laughed. "She can leave a message."

The phone rang again.

"Please, I have to talk to her," Carrie said.

Jake forced Carrie's hand with his between her legs. "Later," he said, and the phone rang once more and Carrie pressed her thighs together and the phone stopped ringing and she started to cry. "Damn you," she sobbed. "God damn you. It's this type of thing that finished us. Now please, if you really care about me, let go of me and get out of here."

For a moment there wasn't a sound in the apartment other than Carrie's quiet sobs, and then Hannah's voice, amplified through the answering machine, broke the silence. "Carrie? Where are you? Call me when you get a chance. I have to stay after five and need a favor of you."

"So Hannah got the day off?" Jake said, squeezing Carrie's hand tighter as he began to rub his fist between her legs. "And it wasn't Mom after all." He pressed his mouth over her ear and whispered, "Stop stalling and give Jake Hornbeck a chance to change your life."

Carrie thought if only he could, but this wasn't what she had in mind. As she began to tell him no he let go of her hand and she heard the sound of his zipper. "What are you doing?" she screamed.

"Enjoy the moment," he said. "It'll beat the hell out of internet dating. You'll see."

Carrie looked at Jake's face in the mirror. His eyes were narrow and dark and bright. The man with the angular face and large brown eyes that she'd found so handsome the first time she met him now looked like a giant rat. Again she told him to leave, that he was out of control, that she hated him, that he wasn't the kind of man she'd thought he was, but his arm seemed to tighten even more across her chest and his fingers dug into her rib cage like some gigantic claw.

She forced out, "Please, I can't breathe."

"Nice and easy," he said, and she felt him press himself between her legs.

She tried to scream for him to stop but his free hand closed over her mouth before she could say anything. She felt as if she were suffocating, the pressure on her chest and his hand over her mouth making it difficult for her to draw anything but short, quick breaths through her nose and then she felt him press hard against her as he moved up between her buttocks.

"Oh, my God, no!" she screamed and reached in the sink, grabbed the blow dryer and whipped it back over her shoulder with all her strength, its oval open end hitting him above the eye with a loud crack.

"You cunt!" he yelled and covered his eye with his hands.

Carrie turned and pushed him backward, relieved to be free of his grasp. Jake took his hands from his eye and looked at the blood on them. "You're just like all the rest," he said. "Want it on your terms, or not at all." He dangled his arms and bent forward at the waist, blood dripping down his cheek to the floor. The crazed smile returned to his face. "Well, I'll teach you a lesson you'll never forget." He began nodding as though he was agreeing with some internal voice. "Run off to Alaska with some stranger if you must, but no bitch like you turns Jake Hornbeck down." And he came at her, bent at the waist, his pants sliding to his ankles, his penis erect.

Carrie swung the hair dryer at him but he blocked the blow with his forearm, jolting the dryer free from her grasp, sending it caroming across the floor. He smiled, straightened slightly and grabbed her shoulders and pulled her against him.

For an instant Carrie's mind went blank, giving in to a blackness of despair. Instinctively she brought her knee up between his legs and felt it make contact with him, felt his grip loosen on her shoulders and watched as he took a step backward and then a second, clutching himself, and dropped to his knees and fall to his side on the bathroom floor and kick his bare feet, his blue jeans and skivvies knotted around one ankle.

Carrie reached down and pulled her towel from beneath his legs. She could hear him groaning and muttering, "You cunt. You fucking cunt."

She ran to her bedroom and wrapped the towel around her and crossed her arms across her bruised chest to warm herself and grabbed her cell phone and dialed and cupped her hand around the phone and whispered, "Hannah Hall, please."

When Hannah finally got on the line, Carrie was sobbing.

"Who's calling, please?" Hannah said.

Carrie tried to muffle her cries.

"Hello? Who's calling please?" Hannah asked again.

Carrie sucked in a breath and let it out and struggled to be understood. "It's me."

"Jesus, are you all right?"

"Come home, Hannah."

"Okay, Carrie, calm down. What's the matter?"

"He tried to rape me."

"Who's he?"

"Jake."

"I thought that was over," Hannah said. "Where is he now?"

"In the bathroom."

"In the bathroom?"

"Rolling around on the floor, holding his balls." Carrie lowered her voice. "I kneed him."

"Jesus, Carrie, when will you …" Hannah stopped before giving Carrie the lecture she knew she deserved. "Call the cops. I'll be home in fifteen minutes, no more."

Carrie nodded at the phone.

"Do what I say for once, will you?" Hannah said.

She nodded again. "Hurry, Hannah," she said, punched off the phone, and stared through her bedroom door into her apartment. Suddenly it didn't look at all like home. She was trapped. Nothing was right. Nothing, and she pleaded to God to get her out of this mess without any more trouble.

She kept the phone in her hand and tiptoed to the bathroom and peeked in. Jake was on his knees with one hand on the side of the toilet bowl, the other pressing a wad of toilet paper against the cut above his eye. His face was streaked with blood and mucous dripped from his nose into the bowl.

Carrie mustered all the courage she could. "I just called the cops, so if you don't want me to squeal on you you'd better get out of here right now."

Jake stood and worked his way into his undershorts and pants and pushed by her into the living room where he shooed a large cat from the couch and pulled a polo shirt and a pair of Tevas from under one of its cushions. He slipped his shirt over his head, struggled to get his arms into the sleeves and slid his feet into his sandals and smoothed their straps closed. "Don't think you've heard the last of me, because you haven't," he said. "I'll get even if it's the last thing I do."

Carrie shook her head. "If you ever bother me again and don't give me back my key, so help me God, I'll tell the cops it was you."

Jake told her to go fuck herself and took the key from his pants pocket and threw it at her and slipped through the door, slamming it behind him.

Carrie collapsed on the couch, wrapped herself tightly with a throw she pulled from the back of it and screamed, "Jesus, it's cold in here!" The cat jumped into her lap and began to purr. She smoothed a trembling hand over the cat's black and white-striped back. "He knows where I live, Alcatraz. Where I work. He knows everything about me." She held the cat close to her and rubbed her cheek against the soft fur of his neck. "But maybe he's in more trouble than I am. Maybe he's worried about me squealing to the cops. Who knows?" She sighed. "All I know is, I want out of here and all I *want* to know is why is it I can't get anything right?"

2

LATER THAT SAME DAY Hannah returned to their apartment a second time. Her first visit had been to comfort Carrie but now as she dropped her purse on the kitchen counter, her tone was impatient and resigned as she called, "Time for a little talk."

She looked Carrie up and down as she wandered into the kitchen wrapped in a large white towel, her tanned skin still moist from a shower. Hannah shook her head. "Cripes, Carrie, hair and nails done just like every other ..." She gestured to her to come close and wrapped her arms around her broad, warm back and held her tight. "Are you all right?" she asked.

Carrie nodded, her cheek moving against Hannah's. "I think so," she whispered. "I'm trying to put it out of my mind. To forget Jake. Forget this place. To move on."

Hannah held Carrie for a moment longer and then eased away from her. "Okay," she said, "what did you tell the cops?"

Carrie looked at the floor. "Nothing."

"Nothing?" Hannah said.

Carrie pulled her hands free and told her that she hadn't called the police, that it was more complicated than Hannah had made it out to be. "It wasn't *that* big a deal," she said. "A close call, but that's all. And part of it was my fault; I've let him get away with stuff like that in the past." Carrie began to cry. "And I didn't want to complicate my life any more than it is already. Calling the cops would have led to lawyers and court appearances and I'd have been a prisoner here forever and that's the last thing I want. It was just something between Jake and me, kind of the final act of a rough relationship. Besides, he thinks I called the cops and wouldn't dare try anything more."

Hannah sighed. "Let's hope you're right. It's your call, Carrie. Your call and your ass but listen to me: Tell your Alaskan adventurer you'll meet him some other time and stay home tonight and get your emotional shit together."

Carrie looked down at the floor and rubbed one bare foot on top of the other. "But, Hannah, I've waited so long to meet this guy. Something about the things he writes feel so right. I'm really looking forward to—"

"Meeting the man of your dreams? The trouble is you *always* think you've just met the man of your dreams. It wasn't just Jake you got wrong. It was that surfer from Hawaii with the hair down to his ass and the guy from Microsoft with the purple Jag ragtop and the piano player from New York and—"

"Are you through?" Carrie said.

Hannah moved her hands as though she wasn't sure and then nodded.

"Then help me," Carrie pleaded, "and tell me why I can't get it right because it seems it's just out of my reach; that if I tried just a little harder, I could do it."

"Sorry to be such a hard-ass," Hannah said and reached for one of Carrie's hands. "No matter what, nothing gives a guy the right to sneak into our apartment and force himself on you, so for God's sake be careful with this new guy. *Really* careful. It's one thing to e-mail back and forth with some smooth-talking stranger; it's a whole 'nother thing to actually meet him."

"I'm trying to sort it all out," Carrie said. "Honest to God I am, so let me try to do this on my own. Okay? Things aren't going to change if I sit around and wait for something to happen. I've got to make it happen myself."

Hannah shook her head in disapproval, then rubbed her hands up and down Carrie's arms. "Okay, but promise you'll be careful? Really careful. Promise me that?"

Through her tears, Carrie promised she'd be careful.

AT 8:30 THAT NIGHT, worrying that she was ignoring Hannah's advice, something that always made her uneasy because Hannah was always right, Carrie left her apartment wearing her favorite maroon mini-skirt and cream-colored silk blouse cinched tight above her hips by a thick black patent leather belt that matched her flat pumps, and headed for her favorite singles bar, the bar that Hannah disapproved of so, but the place where Carrie had dated many of the men and made friends with many of the women, all of whom were searching for the same thing as she.

She arrived before the crowd began to gather and sat alone at a small round table. She ordered an Absolut and tonic and stared out the big street-front window when a tall, graceful stranger, made taller by shiny black cowboy boots, pressed his forehead to the window and cupped his hands beside his eyes to cut the glare. She noticed his hands first, coarse and powerful but somehow—she couldn't explain how—comforting. When he looked directly at her, she felt her face flush and looked away. When she dared look back, he mouthed, "Carrie?"

She nodded quickly and whispered, "Bart McFee?" Her heart began to race. The stranger pulled away from the window, the heels of his palms leaving crescents of moisture on the glass. He smoothed his dark ponytail, then placed his hands together in prayer and a boyish smile crossed his face. She couldn't help but smile, too, then thought, no, you silly goose that's not being careful; that's not the new Carrie Ritter. And for an instant she wondered if it was too late to change her mind but, as the stranger pushed open the door and walked toward her, she thought she would explain it all to Hannah by telling her that the closer he got the more drop-dead gorgeous he became, even though she knew Hannah would simply add, "Haven't they all?"

But it wasn't just his looks that made Carrie think maybe he was the one. It was the gentle way he put out his strong-looking hand and said, "It's not too late to change your mind." She was surprised he knew what she'd been thinking and that made her relax a bit but also scared her because she wondered who would want to be around someone who knew what you're thinking—even feeling—maybe even before you did? But she took his hand and said, "No, please," and wondered what sort of a greeting that was.

Bart smiled at her and placed his hands on the back of the stool. "Good, but from all our e-mails I thought I knew almost all there was to know about you, but—"

"But what?" Carrie said. "Is something wrong?"

Bart laughed. "Just the opposite. From the way you described yourself, I kind of expected a...well...a...a big, strong Iowa farm girl. But you're beautiful. Absolutely beautiful."

Again Carrie felt her face flush. Something told her that this stranger meant what he said. She smiled. "But there are lots of things you don't know about me either, so please don't think I've told you everything."

"Nor me," Bart said, "but that's part of the adventure; part of the mystery."

Carrie thought an adventure sounded romantic and was titillated by the idea of a mystery; that they were exactly what her dull, predictable life needed when Bart asked if she'd like to try an Alaskan drink, a Love Me Tender.

Carrie said she'd *try one*. She was trying to be firm, be careful, but while Bart was at the bar she promised herself that if it didn't work out this time, that this was the last time, for none had ever led to the man of her dreams, although there had been a couple of close calls.

She drew a deep breath and told herself to keep her head about her and not do anything stupid, to keep it all in order and go slow. She took another deep breath and wondered how this gorgeous stranger was making out with the odd-sounding drinks. As she turned to look he was walking toward her with an easy swagger, and she thought he was built just like her—big hands and feet, narrow hips and broad shoulders—but on him it looked right. Better than right. When Bart saw her looking at him he smiled and she thought it was a friendly smile, not a smile filled with lechery like so many other smiles she'd seen so many times in this bar, and she relaxed a bit.

And then she saw him. She felt a tightness in her chest and her breath came in warm, heavy bursts. Jake Hornbeck was following Bart. He was smiling the smile that she knew led to trouble. He wouldn't try anything in public or would he? Wasn't he worried about the cops?

Bart slid a glass in front of her and sat. Carrie forced a smile and coughed out, "Bart, do you know this guy?"

"What guy?"

She lowered her voice. "The guy behind you, with the bandage above his eye."

Bart looked over his shoulder, but before he could answer, Jake said, "Well, if it isn't the fickle Carrie Ritter and her internet ticket to Nowheresville, Alaska."

"Go away," Carrie said, "Please." She looked at Bart for help, but he didn't move, his big hands wrapped around his glass, his emotionless stare fixed on the table.

"Go away? Up until today you couldn't get enough of me, or don't you remember?" He placed a hand on Bart's shoulder. "Maybe it's because I can't take you away from it all like this poor sucker."

Carrie knew at that instant that she should have called the police and prayed that Bart would somehow help her. But she thought there was no reason for him to do anything, that she was nothing more than a stranger whom he'd met through the internet, and she mustered all the courage she could and looked up at Jake and forced herself to focus on his narrow-set, dark eyes. "Enough's enough, Jake. It's over."

Jake shook his head, his eyes filled with the same wild, animal-like look they'd had in her bathroom that morning. "It's not going to be that easy."

Without looking up, or turning to face him, Bart said quietly, "Please, let the lady alone."

"Please, let the lady alone?" Jake looked at Carrie. "Who is this guy? Mister Manners?"

Carrie had no idea how to answer. Or even if she should. She looked to the gorgeous man seated close to her for help, but all she saw was a stranger and realized how alone she was, and a chill ran through her.

Bart raised his eyes to her and smiled a comforting smile. He looked over his shoulder at Jake and then beckoned to the bouncer. "Okay. Let's skip the formalities. Time's up. Leave the lady alone."

When Bart spoke, people at the nearby tables stopped talking and stared at Jake and him. Two women seated at the table nearest them picked up their drinks, pushed their stools back and moved away. Carrie held her glass so tightly to stop her hands from shaking that she thought she'd break it, but all she could think of at that moment was how nice 'leave *the lady* alone' sounded when Jake said, "Shove it up your ass."

Carrie watched Jake's *Death Before Dishonor* tattoo swell with each rhythmic flex of his biceps and thought of his super-human strength. Suddenly she didn't want to be in this singles bar causing this handsome stranger to be hurt because she never could get things right. Her plan to change her life already was headed in the wrong direction and as usual Hannah had been right, she should have stayed home and gotten her emotional shit together for she could feel things were unraveling at a rapid pace and, once again, she was losing control.

"It'll take a bigger man than you to do that," he said. "But not tonight."

With that, Jake wrapped his arms around Bart's neck and jerked him from his stool, sending it crashing to the floor, the bar going quiet, except for a series of scraping sounds as people pushed their stools from their tables and hurried away.

"Jake, no!" Carrie yelled.

Jake glanced at her and pulled Bart's head down to his hip. Bart's face turned red and the vein in his temple thickened. "So this is the pussy you ditched—"

But Jake never got to finish. A man more than a half-a-foot taller than him with a large, shiny shaved head and a baseball bat grabbed him by the ear and pushed the bat under his nose. "Hit the road, pal," the man said. "You want to fight, join the Marines."

Jake let go of Bart and took a step back. He sized up the bouncer and his baseball bat and raised his hands above his shoulders. "You win this one, fat boy," he said, and then looked at Carrie. "But we're not through. No one gets away with shit like this with Jake Hornbeck." And then, as suddenly as he had appeared, he pushed through the crowded bar and out on to the street and was gone.

Bart rolled his head and stretched his neck. He smiled and lifted his glass toward the bouncer and thanked him for his help.

"Comes with the territory," the bouncer said. He tapped Bart on the shoulder with his bat and nodded at Carrie. "But you two be careful. I've seen a lot of rotten apples in this job and something tells me that guy's trouble. *Real* trouble."

They sat without speaking as though they were weighing the bouncer's comments. Carrie was very much aware of the stares of others in the bar and hurried to finish her drink, thinking she had to get free from all of this, that once again she'd made a terrible mistake.

Once outside Bart put his arm around her and led her to the path along the beach and asked, "What was that all about?"

"You don't really want to know," she said.

Bart nodded and took his arm from her waist, and she wished he hadn't although she couldn't tell if it was because she was frightened by Jake and needed someone to help keep her together, or if there was something special about Bart's touch. Either way, she missed the feeling and asked him if he'd mind putting his arm around her for a little while longer. She couldn't believe what she'd just said and felt her face flush with embarrassment and the warm push of gin and peach vodka from the strange Alaskan drink and quickly added, "I'm a bit shaky right now."

Bart smiled and slipped his arm around her and they walked in silence watching the waves of the Pacific break and spill over the sand. Finally, Bart asked again, "Who was that guy?"

Carrie bit her upper lip and looked at Bart. "He's just a guy I used to date and we've had a pretty rough falling out."

"Got that, but how'd he know about me? About Alaska?"

Carrie took Bart's arm in her hand, held it tightly and drew a deep breath. She didn't want to start off their relationship with a lie; after what she'd just put him through she felt she owed him the truth. "I used you as an excuse to break up with him. He scared me so; I didn't know what else to do." She paused and pleaded for him to understand. "I'm sorry. Really, really sorry. I never thought it would get you—"

"It's okay," he said, and pulled her closer against him. "They all end up like that?"

"No," Carrie said, and laughed a little laugh of relief because they were moving away from Jake, and stammered, "Well … yes … sometimes … but no … never *that* bad." She tried to get the spotlight off herself by asking, "What about you? How do yours end up?"

"They tend to start well but something always seems to go wrong."

"Like what?" Carrie asked.

"I'm too much of a loner for most women." Bart looked away from her. "That and some other stuff cost me a marriage."

Carrie tried to appear as unfazed as possible as she asked, "You're divorced?" She wondered what else he hadn't told her in his e-mails. What other surprises were in store.

Bart stopped walking and took his arm from her waist. "Now I owe *you* an apology. I thought if I told you that I'm divorced you'd never have agreed to meet me. Have I screwed this up before we even got started?"

Carrie looked into his gray eyes, eyes that made her think that maybe she could dream a little, and thought, not by a long shot, but didn't tell him so. "Not yet," she said and asked him what else he hadn't told her.

"Okay. Full disclosure," Bart said. "Married at thirty, divorced by thirty-three."

"Kids?"

Bart looked away again. "Nope. One of the reasons we split." He looked back at her. "How am I doing so far?"

"Not too bad," Carrie said. "But another thing you never made clear: what is it, exactly, that you do for a living?"

"I used to teach. Now I'm kind of a …I don't know… some say I'm a fugitive from society; others say I'm running away from a bad marriage and some other stuff. I'd just say I'm a self-styled adventurer who spends most of his time in Alaska." They walked in silence for a moment when Bart said, "Well, how do you feel about Alaska?"

"What about it?" she said.

He shrugged. "It's the place I call home, Carrie. I only come back here on occasion to tidy up loose ends. Alaska's what I love. Where I'm at peace, where I'm headed in a few weeks."

"And you think I should go with you? Just run off to Alaska, just like that?"

"I'm only asking you to think about it," he said. "From your e-mails I think you'd love it. Besides it would get you away from that Jake guy and it might be the solution to all your other problems."

"All my problems?" Carrie hadn't expected the invitation to be focused on what was best for her. It caught her off guard and scared her. She had been so open with Bart in their e-mails about her dead-end situation, and now she was being asked to put her money where her mouth was. Was it just idle chatter or was she really ready for a change—an adventure, a mystery—and a dramatic one at that? She needed time to gather her thoughts, time for the vodka and the gin to loosen their grip. "Problems?" she said again. "What problems?"

Bart hooked his arm around her waist and kept walking. "I know this is scary stuff and will take a lot of guts…" Carrie didn't hear what he said next for again she wondered how this stranger seemed to know what she was thinking and feeling almost before she did. "But I can promise you that living in the Alaska outback will be new as new can be and far from boring. It may not lead anywhere, but it may help you discover where you want to go. That's one of the beauties of living off the grid. It clears your mind and can cleanse your soul as well." For a second he tightened his grip on her waist. "Worse comes to worse, Carrie, it's only for a few months."

The fact that it would only be for a little while gave her comfort, and the idea of spending time with this gentle, gorgeous man who seemed to put her needs and feelings before all else led her to believe that maybe—just maybe—she'd finally got it right.

"Well?" he said. "What do you think?"

"We'll see," Carrie said. "We'll see. I need to know lots more about it, and you, and time to think it over."

THEY SAID GOODNIGHT at the foot of her apartment steps standing like two awkward teenagers and looking at one another for a long while without speaking. Carrie could feel her heart beating until Bart finally took her face in his hands and kissed her. When they parted, he asked if he could come in.

Carrie quickly raised her hands to hold him in place and said, "Not tonight," and then softened her tone. "I know I'm giving you a mixed message but at times I get confused about what's right and what's wrong, and this is one of those times. I need some time to pull myself together. It's not you. Please try to understand. It's been a really bad day—a *really* bad day—and I'm confused about a lot of things, including Alaska."

Bart smiled down at her, took her by her shoulders and said he understood; that it was okay, that everybody has bad days and that he hoped she'd give Alaska serious thought.

She scolded herself to be careful—to take it slow—but as Bart walked away she could still imagine his gray eyes and gentle smile, feel his strong hands and taste his kiss. "Bart, wait," she called out.

Bart stopped and turned. He shook his head as though he knew what she was about to say. "Not to worry, I'll call tomorrow."

"Promise?"

He smiled. "Promise. Now, get a good night's sleep. It'll do you good."

The calm, kind manner in which he answered told her that he was a man of his word, that he had everything in order while she was spinning out of control; that he might be just right for her, that maybe they could be fugitives from society for a while. But Alaska? Why Alaska? And then she thought, Why not? Maybe he's right. Maybe it would solve all her problems. Clear her mind. Cleanse her soul. Be an adventure. Be what she needed.

3

THE WOLF SET OUT ALONE with nothing to remind him of his origins and his crowded natal pack but the tracking collar he had worn ever since researchers from The Department of Fish and Game had drugged him with a dart shot from a helicopter, studied him and entered him on their capture data sheet as GW027, Gulkana wolf #27. He was recorded as a 105-pound, black and buff *canis lupus*, measuring six feet from the tip of his nose to the base of his tail. His age, based on the whiteness and slight wear of his teeth, was estimated at two years. But now, two months after his profile had been programmed into Fish and Game's database in Anchorage, the file on GW027—nicknamed Daredevil by the wildlife biologists who had captured and eventually released him—was being closed out because the mortality sensor on his radio tracking collar indicated that, in all likelihood, GW027 had been killed.

Daredevil had begun his dispersal seventy miles northwest of the town of Gulkana and worked his way south, keeping the snow-covered peak of Mount Wrangell at his left shoulder. The afternoon he crossed Route Four near Glennallen would be the last time he would cross a road with the sun high above him. It was then that he learned to be wary of the trucks that carried fresh-hewn, sweet-smelling spruce and cedar logs south to Valdez and west to Anchorage, at first hearing the hissing and barking of airbrakes and then the report of a high-powered rifle as the gravel by his muzzle sprayed in front of him.

He leapt to the thick undercover, running from a second loud crack, covering ten yards with each bound; running and running to the edge of the Copper River where he splashed in its shallows until the water flowed above his long forelegs. There he stopped in a small, clear backwater, pricked his ears and worked his leathery black nostrils. Minutes passed before he was satisfied that danger was not following him or about him. He lowered his head and drank from the river and, when his heart had slowed to its normal rate, waded from the water and investigated an abandoned den that had been dug out of a low rise overlooking the river, its entrance littered with wolf scat and gnawed sticks and the bleached bones of beavers, snowshoe hares and caribou calves. He crawled to the back of the flea-infested shelter and crouched most of the night without sleep, watching and scenting for his mysterious new enemy.

TWO DAYS LATER Daredevil worked his way southeast toward the town of Chitina and the junction of the Copper and Chitina Rivers when he was stopped by a curious scent. He stood hidden in a stand of spruces, searching, listening and scenting for trouble until the June sun slipped behind the mountains, throwing its soft nighttime glow across the lowland grasses and waving spikes of reddish-pink fireweed. He could not wait for darkness to continue his hunt, for this time of year darkness never came. He could only rely on the shadows of the low sun and his keen senses of hearing and smell. He dropped his body flat to the ground and crawled into the open, stopping every few yards and raising his head. Finally, he stood, the fresh scent still beckoning. He sensed no danger.

He crept through the tall grass when suddenly something foreign to him clenched his right foreleg with a loud slap. A crippling pain ran up his shin to his shoulder. He yelped and jumped back, pulling the trap chain taut. He stared at the trap and growled. He pulled his leg again and the skin of his shin peeled down to shiny white bone and bright-colored blood ran freely to his large forepaw, but his leg did not come free. He held his ground and tried lifting, then pulling his leg, furiously biting at the steel jaws of the trap. He jerked his leg and attacked the trap a second time. Nothing changed except the pain grew hotter, more intense, his blood now covering his once-buff-colored paw.

The wolf stood still for a moment; his head cocked to one side as though he were trying to find the answer to this puzzle and then lowered his head and lay down. Thick, glistening strands of drool and his long pink tongue hung from his mouth. His heart pounded rapidly and he huffed loud breaths that tasted sour to him. He whimpered and closed his eyes. He had made his second mistake in as many days— and perhaps his last. The freedom he had known all his life had ended.

WITHIN A FEW HOURS the sun crept above the foothills of the Wrangell Mountains and another long day began. Daredevil licked his wound clean and lay with his ears flat to his head, his foreleg throbbing with pain. The sound of a twig snapping caused him to stand and face the woods. Again he pulled his leg to free himself from danger, growling and straining at the trap, but the trap held him in place, and in pain. He saw movement in the trees and then his enemy stepped into the open and stopped when their eyes met.

The native Alaskan who stood at the edge of the forest was an Ahtna boy in his early teens. His wide-set eyes, long nose and broad mouth resembled his noble Ahtna ancestor, Chief Goodlataw, and the elders in his tribe had named him Littlelataw, a name he carried with great pride until his reputation as a boy who exaggerated his secret experiences while hunting earned him the name Storyteller. He held a crude bow and wore mud-caked running shoes, faded blue jeans and a camouflage shirt cinched at his waist by a frayed leather belt. A large bowie knife hung loosely from the belt, the point of its scabbard almost touching the boy's knee. A Spruce grouse and a mallard duck, its iridescent green head flashing in the low sunlight, hung by their necks from a piece of twine the boy had looped over one shoulder; over his other he had slung a narrow canvas quiver that held a handful of arrows.

At the sight of the boy the wolf pulled back his lips, baring his large, curved incisors, let out a low growl, and lowered his shoulders and backed away, once again trying to pull his leg free from the blood-covered steel. When he could move no further the animal straightened and stared at the boy, his hackles raised in a thick black mass between his shoulders and his ears and tail pointed skyward in an attempt to appear as large and threatening as he could.

"Holy shit," Storyteller said. He had never seen a live wolf this close before and the sight caused his heart to beat rapidly.

Daredevil continued to growl and kept his eyes on the boy's.

Storyteller walked slowly into the meadow, keeping a safe distance from the wolf. He took a step toward the animal and again the wolf tried to back away. He took another step forward and Daredevil lunged at him, the trap holding him in place. The boy jumped back, and then shook his head. "You're not going anywhere."

He stepped twice more until he was a body-length from the wolf. He set his bow and the mallard and the grouse in the grass and sat, cross-legged. He slid two arrows from the quiver, placed them in his lap and folded his hands across his stomach, one hand gripping the handle of the bowie. He took in and let out a deep breath and after a moment closed his eyes and bowed his head. His coarse black hair, kept in place by a red and white bandana knotted at the back of his head, fell forward on his shoulders. He pulled the bandana tight and ran his hands back over his hair and then sat still as though he had fallen asleep. The only sound in the meadow was his breathing mixed with the wolf's.

When Storyteller looked at the wolf again, Daredevil was lying on his belly in the matted grass, his head upright, his ears laid back. He was panting quietly. "Okay, brother," the boy whispered, "we begin."

For a moment, the Ahtna did nothing but keep his eyes on Daredevil's and nod slowly to him, drawing and releasing heavy breaths. The wolf whimpered, lowered his head and switched his bushy tail. The boy then took an arrow in each hand and raised them in front of his face and began to tap them across each other. "Look at your brother," he commanded in a quiet voice. "Trust him." He continued to tap the arrows but did not speak until the wolf's almond-shaped eyes began to close.

"Trust your brother," he said again and then chanted in rhythm with the clicking of the arrows. "Rest, like a cloud. Softly … softly … silently … silently."

The boy's cadence slowed. He lowered his voice further.

"Listen to your brother. Listen to your spirits."

Moments passed and the wolf's eyes closed and he lay on his side. His tongue dropped from his jaw and curled in the dirt. His thick tail thumped once in the grass.

"Trust your brother and no harm will come to you."

The boy closed his eyes but continued to tap the arrows, more slowly, more quietly, until their clicks were no louder than the call of a cricket.

After a moment of silence, Storyteller opened his eyes, laid the arrows beside him and rested his hands in his lap. He paused and then whispered, "Trust your brother. He trusts you."

He placed his hands on the ground in front of him and knelt forward but the wolf did not stir and the boy reached for the springs of the trap and struggled to open its powerful jaws. Daredevil lay still, his rib cage rising and settling in a slow, steady fashion; his wound caked with blood and dirt; green-headed flies buzzing and sitting on the blackened, matted blood.

Storyteller stared at the wolf's bloody forepaw and laid the fat of his copper-colored hand beside it. The paw was broader than his hand and, although he had seen wolves' tracks in the mud and snow many times before, he shook his head in wonderment.

He slid the bowie from its scabbard and reached for the wolf's throat. "Trust your brother," he said. "He will set you free." He slipped the broad blade under the radio collar and cut at it until it fell away from the wolf's neck and lay curled in the grass. "There," he whispered. "You're free as the thunder that rolls in the mountains."

The boy leaned back on his haunches, sat erect and set his hands on his knees, the glittering bowie still tight in his grip. His heart was beating as hard as he had ever felt it, but he could not contain the smile on his thin lips. "I will not tell anyone our story," he said, "for they would just laugh at me."

He stood, put up his knife and looked down at his brother. "Go now," the boy said. "The spirit of Littlelataw will always be with you."

Storyteller picked up his bow, quivered his arrows, returned to the wolf and laid the grouse and the duck in front of him. He re-set the trap, tripped it with an arrow to leave his sign, and then walked toward the edge of the woods where he stopped. "Go on, git!" he yelled, and disappeared into the trees.

The wolf stood and pulled his injured forepaw to his chest and then set it carefully on the ground and took a hobbled step. He limped in a circle around the trap and then lifted his leg and made water and sniffed the dead birds and tore into them, coughing and spitting feathers as he ripped the skin free from the birds' carcasses. When he was through eating, he stared at the trap and his surroundings and limped into the forest. As he disappeared into the undercover, he and the boy left a puzzle for the trappers who later would come upon the scene: their bloody trap holding nothing but a single arrow and a few buff hairs of a wolf's foreleg; a pile of grouse and mallard feathers blowing about in the matted grass; and a Fish and Game GPS radio collar lying nearby, cut cleanly in half.

DAREDEVIL MOVED CAUTIOUSLY, hunting only in the shadow hours of the day, nursing his wound frequently, following the gray Chitina River as it flowed lazily southeast. In two days' time he climbed through a pass beneath Castle Peak and worked his way toward the small settlement of McCarthy until the man-scent drove him south again into the shadows of Sourdough Peak. He forded the Chitina River there and continued south toward the remains of the abandoned Bremner Gold Mine, giving wide berth to its dilapidated wood-frame buildings and rusted-out Ford trucks, and turned east again, toward the distant Bagley Icefield, its sea of snow and ice glowing a crystal blue in the summer light. Three hundred miles from his natal pack he stopped west of the Chitina and Logan Glaciers, the Yukon Territory stretching to the east, British Columbia to the south, and began to urinate on trees, defecate on rocks and rub his sleek body against prominent landmarks to create scent posts that would mark his new territory—his new home.

He stood in the shade of birch trees, protecting himself from the building heat of the morning sun and surveying the grassy meadow in front of him, his yellow, slyly curved eyes blinking with sleep. Once assured that he was safe, he walked along the fallen birch trunk he was standing on, stepped off it and began to search for a shaded spot to lie down and sleep.

His bed once selected, he stretched his forepaws in front of him and moved them close together, lowered his front shoulders until his keel-like chest rested on the grass. He let out a low grunt as he stretched his long frame and then turned in a tight circle a number of times and lay down. For a moment he closed his eyes, his tail folding the grass as it swept slowly from side to side, and then he rolled over and pushed his legs stiff above him, the wound on his foreleg a hairless, glossy pink where the torn skin had begun to grow together. He worked his muscular frame against the ground to scratch his black and buff, thickly furred back. With each turn of his body he uttered a guttural grunt of ecstasy and finally raised his head and pointed his throat and muzzle toward the snow-capped mountains in the distance, opened his large jaws and howled one husky, resonating howl. Lonely but determined, he was calling for a companion to help him in the hunt, to couple with him and start their pack. He listened for a far-away answer, but the meadows, streams, forest and mountains were silent, and he curled into a tight ball and went to sleep.

4

WEDGED INTO a cramped canvas seat of a de Havilland Beaver, Carrie adjusted a pair of olive drab earphones, careful not to disturb the dark glasses nestled on her tight blonde curls. She stared out the airplane's window, half-dazed, half-amazed by what she was witnessing. She was being transported to the Alaska bush and beginning the adventure with the man she thought—*finally*—might just be the man she'd so desperately been looking for.

As the Beaver's powerful engine droned on, Carrie looked down at a frozen river that shimmered like a silver ribbon on the blackening valley floor as it wandered beneath jagged mountains that climbed above her, their glaciers turning from white and watery blue to copper as the sun settled behind their peaks. Through her headset she heard Bart's reassuring voice: "That's the Chitina River."

Once again it was as though he sensed what she was about to ask, and once more Carrie wondered how this relationship would work out—living with a man who always seemed to know what she was thinking—when Bart pointed to the mountains within her view. "Some of those peaks are 16,000 feet high."

She said it was beautiful and slipped back into her trance until they passed over a small cluster of buildings and, a moment later, over another. She straightened in her seat and tapped a freshly manicured fingernail against the window, her black down mittens swinging freely from the snaps on her parka sleeves. "Bart, what are those?"

"That's the Bremner gold mine right below us. It's been abandoned for years. The bigger settlements were mining towns. They're mostly ghost towns now."

"People actually lived there?"

He turned to her and nodded. "Some still do."

Carrie shook her head in amazement. He had to be kidding; no one could survive out there no matter how badly they wanted whatever it was they were after—gold or no gold.

It was with this thought that she finally began to understand what it was she was undertaking, and her conviction that she was doing the right thing with the right man started to surrender to the thought that she might be doing the single dumbest thing of her young life. She shook her head and watched the vast landscape of trees and the frozen, snow-dusted ponds grow larger and larger as the pilot began his approach to the Wrangell Mountain Expeditions' air strip. The plane began to bounce and rock and her stomach pushed into her throat and she grabbed Bart by the shoulder of his parka and cried, "Sweet Jesus!"

"It's okay, Carrie," he said. "Not to worry, Whitey's done this thousands of times."

The plane rocked and twisted for a few moments more before touching down and skiing to a halt at the end of a snow-covered runway where Whitey switched off the engine. "Just in time, McFee," he said. "Another fifteen minutes and we'd been zero-zero."

"Zero-zero?" Carrie asked.

"Not enough visibility to land," Bart said.

She pulled off her headset and tapped Bart on the shoulder. "But it's not even four o'clock yet. You said the days were short, but how short?"

"When the damn darkness sets in, the sun kind of glows from behind the mountains for a few hours, and that's about it." He patted the sleeve of her bulky down parka. "Don't worry. That only goes on for a few months. You'll love it. You'll see. Where else can you watch the moon rise while you're eating breakfast?"

Carrie stared at Bart, and while she couldn't believe his response, she also couldn't believe the beauty of his chiseled profile, his straight nose and strong-looking jaw. Gorgeous, gentle Bart, she thought, and muttered, "Where else?"

THAT NIGHT Carrie lay with Bart under layers of thick, brightly striped Hudson Bay blankets in blackness the likes of which she'd never experienced. Before sleep began to overtake her, she listened to the wind roll down the snow-packed runway and past their little cabin. Mixed with the wind's screaming, she could hear the lectures Hannah had given her before she left La Jolla, starting with the familiar "when are you ever going to learn?" speech that this time began, "You damn near got raped a few weeks ago and now you're running off to Alaska with a guy you've only been dating for two weeks? Get real, Carrie. Get a grip!"

"But he's not a stranger anymore, and maybe he never was," Carrie had insisted. "I feel like I've known him all my life. And he's so gentle and patient. And he cares about what I think and how I feel. And he's an adventurer. And he's—"

"Gorgeous," Hannah interrupted. "But aren't they all?" She paused and asked again, for what seemed to Carrie like the hundredth time, "But Alaska, Carrie? *Alaska*?"

Carrie argued that the timing was perfect, that she needed a change and Hannah answered that she'd said the same thing the week before. "And the week before that and the week before that."

"But this time it's different, Hannah. I promise. Something tells me Bart's the man I've been waiting for and it's not just because he's so gorgeous. He understands me; knows who I am. I feel trapped here. I need a change. I really do. I'm twenty-nine, my biological clock's ticking, and nothing new ever happens in my life. Nothing. Ever. Please, don't hate me for this but I've got to get out of the rut I'm in and get away from this place for a while."

"Okay, okay," Hannah said, "but running off to Alaska, is that really the best solution to your problems?"

"There's only one way to find out," Carrie answered, hoping she was right. "So, good-bye root canals and lecherous dentists and Saturdays at the mall, and good-bye singles scene." She patted Hannah's hand confidently and smiled. "It's okay. If it doesn't work out, I can always come home."

With that Hannah's tone softened slightly, but she continued to ask questions as if she had a checklist for Carrie that she was determined to complete. "But have you ever wondered why there are tons of single men up there and so few single women? Why Bart had to run an ad to find someone who'd take him up on his crackpot idea?"

"Don't worry—"

Hannah pointed her finger at her. "Because not many women are as restless as you are; that's why. Just listen to this again and listen *carefully*." Hannah read aloud from the Personals section of the San Diego *Union Tribune*: 'Be free again.' She stopped. "Free, my ass, Carrie. Since when is being locked in a log cabin all winter *free*? And you think you're trapped here?" She shook her head. 'White male, 36, college educated, seeks female companion to live back to basics lifestyle in Alaska bush country. Commune with nature. Breathe clean air. Discard financial worries, urban pressures and southern California traffic. Live off the grid. McFeeB@aol. com...' Hannah paused. "What a crock of shit!"

"I don't think so," Carrie said.

"Are you kidding? Do you know what they say about the guys in Alaska?" She didn't wait for an answer. "The odds are good, but the goods are odd. *The goods are odd*, Carrie, and that goes for your gorgeous adventurer."

"Hannah, for once in my life I know what I'm doing," Carrie argued. "Besides, things will never change unless I make them change."

But now, lying in the darkness, the wind shaking the walls of the small cabin, Carrie could see Hannah making her points, each time touching a finger on her left hand with the index finger of her right.

"First, he's already been divorced. Second, he's ten years older than you. Third, he's unemployed."

"Wrong," Carrie said. "Double wrong. He's only seven years older and, besides, everyone's unemployed in the wilderness. Unemployed is what they do."

Hannah closed her eyes and shook her head. "Fourth— and the real topper I might add—he's built a log cabin a million miles from nowhere and you're going to keep him company for an *entire* winter?"

"But, Hannah, we'll read and snow shoe and listen to the wolves and gaze at the stars. Bart says up there the stars look so close you feel you can reach up and touch them."

"That's *all* you'll do? All winter? I don't think you get what 'living off the grid' means." She started with her pinkie finger again. "It means there's no running water—no hot showers—and no flush toilet."

And another finger. "And no electricity. That's living off the grid."

Hannah paused. "Carrie, there's not even a phone, for God's sake. That could pose a real problem for you and what will you do if one of you gets sick, or Bart gets eaten by a bear or something?"

Carrie told her that was all part of the adventure, of "living on the edge," as Bart had put it, but now she felt her heart beating rapidly and found it hard to breathe and asked herself why she hadn't listened to Hannah; why she hadn't stayed home.

Once again she wondered why Bart had wanted her to go with him. It certainly wasn't for her survival skills. Was it because she was the only woman desperate enough to say she would? She reached for him to wake him, to tell him that she'd changed her mind, that she'd made a terrible—typical, Carrie Ritter—mistake. She hesitated, her hand hovering above Bart's shoulder, and then lowered it and placed it over her heavily beating heart. She took a deep breath to quiet herself. She owed it to herself to do this. To get out of her rut, to prove that she could do things on her own, that she was more than people think and better, too. That she can get it right.

She listened to Bart's steady breathing mix with the sound of the wind rushing down the runway, the wind-sounds making her feel as if she was in the middle of some god-forsaken river of snow, and she drew another breath, interlocked her fingers and squeezed her palms together hard, and let air out quietly through her mouth.

She thought, I'll show Hannah.

The wind's screaming seemed to grow louder and more desperate.

And, I'll show Bart, too.

She filled her lungs again and exhaled slowly and promised she would. She laid her hands across her chest and smiled for, if worst came to worst, she could always give it up and go home.

A LITTLE BEFORE first light, Carrie followed Whitey as he carried her bulging duffle bag across the runway and nestled it in the sled that looked like a large toboggan to Carrie. Six huskies—all, Bart had said, rejects from the camp's kennels—were already harnessed to the sled and were curled in the snow to protect their faces and feet. As Carrie approached, one raised its head to look at her, its pale blue eyes squinting to protect them from the swirling snow.

"You're good to go, Miss Ritter," Whitey said. "McFee and I stocked the camp well this summer. You'll need to collect some meat along the way, but you should be fine until the spring."

Bart smiled. "Another walk in the park."

Whitey laughed. "Another *winter*, McFee. Another cold, dark winter. You take care."

The two men embraced and slapped each other on the backs of their large down parkas. Whitey turned to Carrie who forced a smile and shifted her weight from one boot to the other and crossed her arms against her chest to keep warm. "You okay?" he asked.

"It's freezing," she said.

"A little below," Bart said.

She felt a slight twinge of panic. "If it's this cold now and it's only October, what's the weather like in January?"

"It gets down into the twenties and thirties," Bart said.

"But it's that now," Carrie said.

"Twenty or thirty *below* zero," Bart said.

Whitey chuckled as he fumbled for his cigarettes. "It was almost that cold yesterday up at Chandalar Lake." He looked at Carrie, her face clouding over at the thought of thirty-below-zero temperatures, and turned to Bart. "I could fly you in the Beaver, if that would work better for you."

"We'll be fine," Bart said.

Whitey nodded toward Carrie. "You're sure?"

Carrie wanted to hear more about flying into camp, but Bart interrupted her thought. "I'm sure," he said. "Winter is the essence of life in the wilderness and I want Carrie to experience it all."

Whitey took a long drag on his cigarette. "She'll do that," he said. "That's for damn sure," and put out his hand to her.

Carrie shook his hand. "This is it?" she asked. She wasn't prepared for the suddenness of the goodbyes, for such a sudden start to her adventure.

"It's all she wrote," Whitey said. "Enjoy the Riviera."

Oh, my God! It gets to be thirty below zero and it's dark all day long and they joke about it? She slumped in the narrow sled, zipped her parka under her chin and arranged a pile of caribou skins over and around her to protect her from the wind that lifted snow in small, icy clouds around her.

"Ready?" Bart asked.

Again she thought she had something to prove and, again thought she could always come home. She cleared her throat and whispered, "Ready."

Bart walked the line of sleeping dogs and prodded each with the toe of his boot and clucked, "Up you gup. Up you gup." All six stood and shook the snow from their thick fur. The two closest to the sled reared on their hindquarters and snarled at each other before settling down. Bart adjusted the headlamp he'd strapped over his wool cap, stepped on the sled's foot boards, gripped the handle bar with both hands and yelled, "Hike up!"

The dogs barked wildly and strained against the towline. Slowly the sled picked up speed. The swirling snow blinded Carrie, her sinuses bruised by the cold, and she realized that all those things that she imagined only happened in books or on TV or in the movies—whiteouts and avalanches and gangrene and people freezing to death—could happen to her. She slipped on her dark glasses and settled deeper in the sled and knotted her scarf across her nose and mouth and tried to curl up, the way the huskies did, to keep warm. Two days of this? she thought. I'll never make it. Six months of this? What have I gotten myself into?

5

THEY MUSHED ALL DAY and through the night and on into the following day until late afternoon, stopping only to relieve themselves and rest and feed the dogs. They ate energy bars and granola by the mitten-full and exhausted two thermoses of coffee. Bart spoke only occasionally— mostly to urge the dogs on—but every once in a while to ask Carrie how she was doing. Hunkered down in the sled, curled beneath caribou skins and trying to sleep and block out the fact that she was chilled to the bone, that her stomach was knotted with hunger, that she was bleary-eyed with exhaustion, she would answer, "Fine. Just fine," all the while thinking that she had made one of the biggest mistakes of her life, even a bigger mistake than getting involved with Jake Hornbeck.

This thought rolled through her mind—it seemed to her for the thousandth time—until the sun began to slip behind the mountains in the distance and she was jarred out of her icy trance by Bart whoaing the dogs at the edge of a small clearing. He dismounted from the sled and smiled down at her. "Welcome to latitude sixty-one. Home, sweet home."

"Home?" Her spirits were lifted by the news that the interminable trip was over, even though she found it hard to believe that this godforsaken place was what she was to call "home" for the next six to eight months.

"Yes, home," Bart said and then pointed to the mountains. "That long dark blue slide is the Bagley Icefield. The pink one with the flat top is Mount Logan. She's almost 20,000 feet tall and kind of keeps an eye on my place when I'm not here."

What's there to keep an eye on? Carrie wondered as she struggled with the caribou skins to sit up.

"Don't you just love it?" he asked.

His pleading question reminded Carrie of how Bart had described his camp: nestled in a peaceful little meadow there would be a main cabin, with a black stove pipe sticking through the snow on the roof and snowshoes hanging on either side of the door, and a smaller cabin for the sauna. "Quite luxurious," he had said with apparent pride but had warned her that the buildings were small and had even given her the dimensions of the main cabin, quickly adding, "But it's bigger than Thoreau's cabin at Walden Pond, and he lived there for over two years."

At the time it had all sounded so romantic, she guessed because she never gave much thought to the idea of putting an entire house—kitchen, dining room, living room and bedroom—into an area sixteen feet by sixteen feet because she was going to Alaska with her gorgeous, gentle adventurer to start her new life and everything else was secondary. Up until now.

She stepped from the sled and stomped her boots to warm her frozen feet. She took a more careful look about her. "It's just the way you described it," she said in a low voice, but not as she imagined it, for she never would have guessed that early in October the snow would have drifted as high as her waist, nor that there would be wood piled every-where. Everywhere, she thought. Absolutely everywhere.

No, when Bart and she had discussed it, she'd fantasized that fires were for cuddling in front of and snow shoes were for *playing* in the snow. But now, with long blue shadows lying across the snow at her feet and the temperature dropping as quickly as the sun, the stovepipes and the snowshoes and the rows and rows of firewood looked very cold and there was nothing romantic or fun about them.

She studied the scene without speaking, trying to make sense of it all, taking in every detail when the shadow of a large bird flitted over the snow, causing her to flinch. "Don't worry," Bart said. "He means no harm. Quite the opposite, actually. He's a friend."

Carrie couldn't believe what she was hearing: a mountain that looks after his homestead; a bird for a friend. "You've got a *crow* for a friend?" she said. "What kind of place is this anyway?"

Bart smiled. "A raven, actually."

Carrie looked back at the raven. It had settled on a dead branch of a nearby hemlock and stretched its neck, fluffed the ebony feathers of its cape and looked back at her with one bright black eye, its other half-closed and milky white. She took a deep breath and cocked her head to imitate the raven and show Bart that she wasn't intimidated by it all.

With another look about her she noticed the outline of a narrow building hidden a few yards back in the woods. She guessed it was the outhouse—the "two-holer" Bart had called it—and thought she'd freeze her butt off just taking a pee. She stepped through the snow to the front of the cabin where drifted snow pressed against the door. To the right of the door she could make out the frosted, crystallized imprint of an animal's nose on the windowpane. Fresh paw prints were imbedded in the snow on the sill. "Bart, a dog's been looking in your window," she said.

He leaned over her shoulder, set his ski goggles on top of his wool cap and studied the prints. "It's a wolf, and a pretty big one at that."

With the mention of a wolf and the temperature dropping and her surroundings growing darker by the minute, Carrie wanted to get someplace safe and warm and out of the wind and the cold. She was as curious as she was worried about what she would find in the cabin and kicked the drifted snow away from the door, lifted the crude wooden latch and pulled the door open, leaving a smooth fan-shaped pattern in the snow. Her first thought was how ordered the cabin was, but this impression was quickly overtaken by how small—really small—it was. There were only five pieces of furniture, including the woodstove: a mattress resting on a wood frame with a propane lantern hanging above it; a card table with dog-eared copies of *The Norton Anthology of Poetry* and *The Collected Poems of Robert Service* placed on a corner; and two straight-back wood chairs. "That's it?" she said to herself, and shook her head and continued with her inventory, becoming more and more depressed as what was in store for her became clearer and clearer.

Rows of canned goods in cardboard cases were stacked against one wall almost to the ceiling. On top of the tan cases were sacks of flour, rice, beans, onions and sugar, several containers of salt, pepper, baking soda, dehydrated potatoes, dried fruit, and a bottle of vanilla extract.

Two rough-hewn boards braced above the bed were lined with paperback books.

Next to the wood stove were two dozen or so split logs. A large black iron pot and skillet sat on the stove, and a rifle rested on large nails behind it. To the right of the stove a row of small shelves—peppered with mouse droppings—held a few plates, bowls, a small collection of tarnished eating and cooking utensils and a knife with a long, narrow blade and stag horn handle.

A galvanized bucket sat beneath the lone window and two dark-feathered goose wings hung by leather cords from the back of the door.

This is all there is for the next eight months? Carrie stopped herself, thinking she could always get Bart and the dogs to take her back to Whitey and his bouncy little airplane whenever she wanted.

She shuddered and asked Bart to light the stove and the lamps, to warm up her "new home," and couldn't believe she'd called it that. As Bart knelt and set the fire, Carrie noticed two wooden crates protruding from under the bed; one filled with a man's clothes, the other empty. She pointed at the empty crate and asked if it was for her.

Bart nodded.

Carrie stared at him. "How'd you know I'd be coming?" she stammered.

"I didn't."

"But the empty crate—"

"I had to be prepared. Up here—"

"So what did you do? Import the first woman you could find who was crazy enough to join you?" Her spirits were dropping and she was growing edgier with each answer. Once again she could hear Hannah's biting comments.

Bart looked up from the fire. "You know that's not the case, but out here companionship *is* a key to survival—as is being prepared for whatever might come your way."

Carrie tried to speak, but Bart held up a hand to her and smiled. "Not to worry. I was hoping for someone just like you."

Up until that moment she'd thought she was someone special. Tears began to well in her eyes and she scolded herself to hold it together. She didn't know what to say or to think and brushed past Bart, pushed open the door and trudged to the sled, angrily kicking at the deep snow. Darkness was quickly settling around the cabin and, as it did, her new world seemed to grow even smaller. She stared down at the sled, the six dogs now dark figures burrowed deep in the snow. "What have I done?" she cried. "What in God's name have I done?"

She stood for a moment and studied the silhouettes of the outhouse and the sauna and turned quickly at the sound of the raven flapping his wings as he shifted his position in the hemlock behind her. "This is it? For an entire winter?" she said, as though she were addressing the bird. "For you maybe my friend, but not for me."

She pulled her duffle from the sled and dragged it back to the door and, once inside, to the edge of the bed. Already she could feel the heat from the stove begin to take the chill from the cabin. As she knelt and unzipped her bag, Bart took one of the goose wings from the back of the door and swept the small patches of snow that had followed her duffle across the cabin floor out the door. Can't I do anything right? she wondered. She wasn't cut out for this. She was a California girl.

Bart re-hung the goose wing and lifted the rifle from the wall and took a box of cartridges from the shelf behind the wood stove. "Be back in a while," he said.

Carrie used the time alone to organize the clothes that Bart had helped her buy, the first wardrobe she'd ever owned that had been chosen, as Bart had said, "for function over style." At the time she had laughingly dubbed it "the wardrobe of the new Carrie Ritter," only now she didn't think it was so funny. Once again she told herself not to worry, that she could always go out on the dogsled the way she had come in.

As she reached for the last few items in her bag her face flushed when her hand found her blow dryer and her cell phone. She glanced toward the door to make sure she was still alone and quickly zipped her bag shut and pushed it as far back under the bed as she could.

She stood and ran a shiny red fingernail along the books lined above the bed, curious to see what Bart had been reading. For a moment she felt a twinge of guilt, as if she was spying on him, but then thought, don't be silly; he wasn't hiding them. She recognized some of the books—*The Call of the Wild*, *Deliverance* and *Walden*—but there were many others that she'd never heard of and stopped her hand on *In The Lake Of The Woods*. It was a book Hannah had told her she just *had* to read, and Carrie struggled to remember what Hannah had said it was about, and then it came to her that it was the story of a woman who disappears in the wilds of Minnesota and the reader never knows if her husband killed her or what, and Carrie giggled a nervous giggle and thought this couldn't be her story, or could it? She shuddered, but this time not from the cold. As she pushed the book back in its space on the shelf she was startled by the crack of the rifle, again and again, four times in all.

She screamed, "What's going on?" and pushed open the door and called into the darkness, "Bart, what are you doing? Are you okay?"

The rifle barked once more and then all went quiet.

Carrie waited for an answer and then screamed again, "Bart, what's going on?"

Bart's voice was muffled by the drooping, snow-covered branches of the woods. "I'm taking care of the dogs."

"What do you mean, taking care of them?" She grabbed her hair and pulled on her curls. "What have you done?" Had he killed them? He couldn't have. "You didn't shoot them, did you? They're my only way home!" She didn't wait for him to speak. Something told her she already knew the answer. "How could you? I thought ..." She thought he was so gentle and wondered if she'd run away from one mad man to be with another. She never dreamed he could do something like this. "What kind of man are you?" she cried. "Are you going to kill me, too? What have you done to the dogs? To me?"

Bart's dark form emerged from the woods by the outhouse. Carrie backed from the open door as he trudged toward the cabin, the rifle resting on his shoulder, his boots punching holes deep in the snow, a sled dog loping behind him.

"You're a killer," she cried. "They didn't do anything wrong."

"Nor did I," Bart said quietly. "There's no way we could feed them the whole winter." He shifted his weight from boot to boot like a schoolboy in front of his teacher. "I did it for *us* and for them. If we'd kept them all they'd have starved and we would have, too. It's a difficult lesson to accept but an important one: there are certain things you and I must do to stay alive. Shooting them is no different from keeping the wood stove burning or keeping the stream open. What must be done, must be done. I know it seems cold-blooded, but don't think it was easy for me because it wasn't." He reached down and scratched the ears of the sled dog that had followed him and looked up at Carrie. "I saved the blue-eyed one for you."

"Oh, for God's sake," she said, the cold wind beginning to fill the cabin. "I never thought it would be anything like this. Not anything at all." She was both horrified and frightened by his nonchalance. She tried to fight the tears she felt building behind her eyes. "This isn't what I dreamed about, Bart. It isn't at all what I expected. I want to go home. Right now. I've made a horrible, typical-me mistake. Help me, please."

"We'll hike out after the breakup," he said in a matter-of-fact fashion. "I've got a canoe tied up for us to cross the Chitina."

"The breakup?"

"After spring's come and the river's open."

"But that's months away. I want to go home now. Tomorrow. Not in the spring."

She stood in the open door, staring at Bart thinking he wasn't the gentle adventurer she'd wanted to start a new life with but a wolf in sheep's clothing. She felt defeated by it all and couldn't believe that her hours of agonizing over this decision had led to this. She waved a hand at Bart signaling that she couldn't cope with anything more, that she didn't want to hear any more of his unsettling, other-worldly theories or plans. She pulled the door closed in an effort to shut him out of her life and turned and collapsed face down on the bed.

A feeling of panic, mixed with self-incrimination, swept over her as her tears and choking sobs filled the small cabin. She was restless with anxiety but had no place to turn. She found it hard to breathe and felt the walls of the cabin closing in on her. She thrashed on the bed, rolling one way and then the other, kicking her heavily booted feet with each turn. The light from the lanterns was unbearably bright. She squeezed her eyes tight shut to close it all out and pounded the bed with her fists. "First, Jake Hornbeck and now this!" she screamed, and wondered why these events had taken place so close together. Was it purely coincidence? Or was she being punished for something? Or had she simply added another error in judgment to her already long list? One that could lead to a living hell at best, or her demise, at worst.

She pushed herself from the bed, swept up her parka and went outside to get some space—some room to breathe. The wind had begun to howl and the temperature had dropped to below freezing and the snow swirled about her, biting into her face, burning her cheeks and her hands. She hurriedly slipped into her parka and zipped it to her chin, pulled on her mittens and forced herself to take a step away from the cabin, and then another. She peered into the darkness and saw Bart's headlamp moving back and forth in the woods beyond the outhouse. She realized that every step she took led her deeper into the danger of the unknown and hurried back inside where she sat on the bed, again forcing her eyes closed for everything looked too close, too sparse, too crude.

When Bart returned to the cabin he kept trying to put his hand on her shoulder or his arm around her, and she kept yelling at him to get away. "You're going to be okay, Carrie," he said. "I promise. *We're* going to be okay. Just try to relax. Give it some time."

Some part of her desperately wanted to believe him but she couldn't, for if this is what it took to make a new woman out of her, she didn't want it. She wanted her mom and Hannah and her apartment and the beach and all the other things she'd thought she wanted to get away from so badly.

"Some food will do you good," Bart said. "You haven't eaten anything in almost two days." He started to cook a can of Chunky Soup on the woodstove and Carrie thought, that's dinner? That's what four-star dining's going to be like up here? Again she lay on the bed and burst into tears.

Finally, she sat and said, "Bart, you've *got* to get me out of here." She drew a deep breath to center herself. "I need to leave. I'm scared. Panicked. I feel trapped. I've made a mistake—I know it's a typical, stupid-me mistake—and I'm sorry. Really sorry, for you and for me, but there's got to be a way to get me home."

"I understand," he said and handed her a bowl of soup and a tin cup half-filled with vodka. "Things may look different in the morning."

"They may *look* different, but they won't *be* different," she sobbed. "I want out; to get home. This isn't what I'd hoped for. What I wanted."

"Please, give it some time, Carrie. You've only been here a couple of hours. You'll love it. I know you will. You're right for it and it's right for you."

Carrie sipped her vodka and ate her soup. She didn't say a word, simply shook her head in despair. She poured herself a second drink. As always, Hannah had been right, except there were a whole lot of things even she didn't think of, like where do you brush your teeth? That it's a long walk to the outhouse in the snow in the pitch black just to take a pee. Like where do you get a little privacy when you undress, especially when the man in the room has just killed five dogs and reads books about women who disappear in the wilderness and are never heard of again? She couldn't do this, no matter what she had to prove. No matter what she was looking for.

She grabbed her toothbrush, toothpaste and Bart's headlamp, pulled on her parka, walked outside and trudged to the outhouse and peed quickly, her bare hands clumsy-numb from the cold as she tried to pull toilet paper from its roll.

On the way back to the cabin she kicked through a deep drift and brushed her teeth, using a handful of snow to rinse her mouth, and while she found the snow tingling and refreshing, her fingers burned with cold and she swore she'd never go outside again without her mittens and hurried toward the cabin. From a distance it looked warm and comforting, the orange glow of the propane lamps shining through the window and a cloud of pale smoke and an occasional spark drifting upward from the stovepipe into the darkness.

For a moment the wind calmed and she peeked through the window to check on Bart. He was sitting on the bed, his red suspenders tight across his black and white checked wool shirt, cleaning the rifle. The husky lay at his feet looking up at him with its pale blue eyes. She leaned against the door and studied the sky. The stars were brighter than she had ever seen them. She watched her breath form little clouds as she prayed, "Please, God, help me through this. I'm not a bad person, really, and I've never hurt anyone and don't want anyone to hurt me. Please help me find a way out of here. Help me get home. Please. I'll be a good girl."

As she finished her prayer deep in the woods she heard an eerie sound and didn't need Bart to tell her what it was. From the darkness came a long, chilling howl that seemed to float through the night. It was the cry of the wolf that Bart had promised was more scared of her than she was of him, but she quickly pulled open the door and bolted it shut from the inside.

Bart ran an oily rag over the rifle and smiled. "Time to talk?"

Carrie shook her head and forced herself to look at him. "I want to go to bed. And then I want to leave. And soon. And I'm not kidding."

He stood and placed the rifle on the nails over the stove.

"Turn around, please. I'm dressing for bed," Carrie said.

Bart smiled the smile she'd liked so much the day before. "I'll put the dog out. You take your time." He put on his parka and his navy cuff cap, clucked at the husky, and went outside.

Carrie dug through her box of clothes, located one of the flannel nightgowns she'd bought for her adventure and laid it on the bed. Hurriedly she stripped to her underwear and pulled off her thick wool socks. She tested the coarseness and the cold of the wood floor with her bare feet and put her socks back on. She unsnapped her bra and looked at her panties—the special pair of thong panties from Victoria's Secret with *Paradise Found* written squarely on the crotch— and thought, when would she ever learn? She took them off and hid them with her blow dryer and cell phone in her duffle bag and wondered how many other things would join them.

WHEN BART RETURNED Carrie lay on the far side of the bed facing the wall, the heavy blankets pulled over her head. She listened to him put logs in the stove and undress. When he turned off the lamps he crawled into bed and put his hand on her hip. "Go away!" she said and slapped at his hand. "And don't touch me. You're not the man I thought you were."

"I think I am," he said quietly, "but we all do look a bit different up here. I promise to take the best of care of you. You'll see."

"I don't want to see. I want to go home."

She felt Bart roll away from her and was relieved. "Good night, Carrie," he said. "Please, give it some time. There won't be any more surprises."

She pulled the covers from her head and watched the light from the flames in the woodstove dance on the ceiling. She rubbed her feet together. They were warm in her heavy gray socks and she was comforted that at least she wouldn't freeze to death. She closed her eyes and listened to the sad howl of the wolf.

"That's your wolf," Bart said. "He's welcoming you."

My wolf, my ass, she thought. And some welcome. But for a moment she wondered about the wolf, what his life was like. Was he really as lonely and desperate as he sounded? As she was? But she quickly gave into the warmth of the fire and the emotional drain and fatigue from all that had happened since arriving in the wilderness, and fell sound asleep.

6

CARRIE WOKE to the smell of coffee brewing and the crackling of the woodstove. She sat in bed, stretched her arms above her head and looked about the cabin. In the dust-flecked sunlight that angled through its lone window, everything seemed less foreign, more intimate than the night before. At first the welcoming atmosphere surprised her, then irritated her. No matter what, it wasn't welcoming enough to keep her there, not after what Bart had done to the dogs. She swung her feet to the floor, her wool socks insulating her from the cold of the rough wood planks yet reminding her how different this strange place was from her apartment in sunny, warm La Jolla. She dressed quickly—first long johns, top and bottom, a blue synchilla turtle neck, black bib ski pants, and then her heavy insulated boots. This was one hell of a lot of work just to take a pee and she would be glad when it was over. She zipped her wind-proof fleece, grabbed her mittens—thought, don't leave home without them—and readied herself for her dash to the outhouse.

Outside, the wind had died and the sky was a brilliant blue. Carrie slipped on her dark glasses and thought at least she'd brought one thing from her other life—her real life— that was useful, that didn't make her feel like an outsider. She looked about her and, unlike the night before, Mount Logan, the flat-topped mountain that Bart had said kept an eye on his cabin, was no longer pink but now sparkling white. For a moment she stood and basked in the glow of the sun and thought how much she looked forward to getting back to all the warm things she loved in southern California and checked the thermometer by the cabin door. It read 30 degrees but she couldn't understand how she could be warmed by the sun in freezing weather. This place was so different, she thought. It was like being on another planet. As she started toward the outhouse Bart trudged around the corner of the cabin carrying an armful of firewood, followed by the husky. He asked her how she'd slept. She wanted to tell him that she lay awake all night worrying about how she would get home, but told him the truth. "Fine," she said, but quickly added, "but I was exhausted, for God's sake; I hadn't slept for two days."

"So you're doing better?"

"I don't know, Bart, but I doubt it. I just got up and I've got to pee."

Bart smiled. "Okay. I'll get breakfast started and then I'm going to build Lola a house of her own."

"Lola? Any particular reason for that name?"

Bart looked down at the husky who looked up at him as though she knew he was talking about her and switched her full gray tail. "Nope. Just like it, that's all."

Carrie kicked through the snow to the outhouse where she studied a channel of tamped snow leading into the woods. She guessed it was where Bart had dragged the sled dogs. She shuddered at the thought and searched for blood-stained snow but he hadn't left a sign. It was like it never happened. She wondered what sort of a man he was. Good at covering things up and not discussing them, for sure. But what else? She realized she didn't know him nearly as well as she thought she did, and thought that this was one hell of a time to realize that.

When she had finished her business, and had re-snapped and re-zipped her clothes, she pushed open the door, stepped out into the snow and tripped over the husky who lay buried by the entrance. She caught her balance and the dog rolled over on her back and smoothed the snow with her tail. Carrie felt a smile cross her face, the first in over three days, and reached down and stroked Lola's stomach with a mittened-hand. "Waiting for me?"

The sled dog stood on her hindquarters, placed her fore-paws on Carrie's leggings, and then dropped to all fours and loped ahead of her toward the cabin, as though she were leading her in for breakfast. At the cabin the dog pressed her black nose against the door, her thick tail curved in a grace-ful sickle shape over her back. She looked back at Carrie with her washed-out blue eyes and whimpered. Carrie knelt and rubbed the dog's head and thickly furred back, and then wrapped her arms around her neck. The warmth of another living thing pressing against her cheered and comforted her. "Well, well, well, my new friend," she said, "at least one of us girls wants to keep him company."

BART SET TWO MUGS of coffee and plates of powdered eggs on the table. "Want some squaw candy to go with your eggs?"

"Squaw candy?" She wondered if he was trying to be funny or if this was some kind of initiation.

"Smoked salmon," Bart said.

Carrie nodded and started to say something but Bart interrupted her. "I know you want to go home, but you've got to stay. I'll make sure no harm comes to you." He smiled and placed one of his large hands over hers.

She pulled her hand away. "What do you mean I've *got* to stay? And what harm could possibly come to me in this godforsaken wilderness? There's nobody here to hurt me except you."

Bart looked up from his coffee. He looked surprised by her questions. "I mean I really want you to stay. I know settling in here is quite a shock and I should have better prepared you for it. My mistake, but without the sled dogs it would be foolish to try to leave now." He gave Carrie a stern, almost threatening, look. "You're safer staying put. So give it a chance. You owe it to both of us."

"I'm sorry, Bart, but I really want to go home. This is not what I expected. I know I should have known better. It's far more...more serious than I thought it would be. I don't know what got into me but it's not right for me and, what's more, I don't really understand why you're here, either."

Bart stood. "Maybe this will help." He took a book from the shelf above the bed and sat back at the table. "It's the beginning of *Walden* and answers your question better than I ever could." He took a sip of his coffee and began to read:

"*I went to the woods because I wished to live deliberately, to front only the essential facts of life, and see if I could not learn what it had to teach, and not, when I came to die, discover that I had not lived.*" He paused and looked up as if he was waiting for Carrie to say something; perhaps that she understood.

"But you're young, Bart," she said. "You're not going to die any time soon."

Bart shrugged. "Maybe. Maybe not."

Carrie gave him a curious look. Was that what this was all about: a double suicide or something crazy like that and no one would ever know?

Bart inched his finger down the page. "Just a bit more and I'm done: *I wanted to live deep and suck out all the marrow of life, to live so sturdily and Spartan-like as to put to rout all that was not life, to cut a broad swath and shave close, to drive life into a corner, and reduce it to its lowest terms, and, if it proved to be mean, why then to get the whole and genuine meanness of it, and publish its meanness to the world; or if it were sublime, to know it by experience, and be able to give a true account of it in my next excursion.*"

He closed the book and set it on the table. "Does that help?"

"It's beautiful, but that doesn't mean this is right for me," Carrie said.

"I understand, and if you still want to go home after a week, we'll think of something. It won't be any harder to do in a week than it will be now."

Carrie saw gentleness in Bart's eyes and was moved by Thoreau's words: *"If it's sublime, I'd be able to give a true account of it on my next excursion."*

She looked down at her food and began to eat. The smoked salmon was delicious; the coffee strong and hot; the powdered eggs passable. She thought Hannah would have told her she was out of her mind and thought she had every right to feel that way, but she struck a deal with herself, and looked up. "Okay. I've come this far so I'll give it a little while longer. I can't see any harm in staying a few days more. But if I'm going to stay, I want to know about everything you do. And I don't want any more surprises, like murdering the dogs."

"I didn't murder them," he said, and promised there'd be no more surprises and told her that he was happy she'd decided to stay.

"We'll see," Carrie said. "Right now, start with the dogs. What will you do with them?"

"I'll butcher them and store the meat in an old locker behind the outhouse."

"You killed them and then you'll chop them up? Like all those serial killers and whackos you see on TV? That's crazy stuff."

"I'd be crazy if I didn't," Bart said. "They'd have starved to death. Now, there should be enough to feed Lola almost all winter."

"She'll eat her friends?" Carrie gasped. "That's the sickest thing I've ever heard."

"She's a dog, Carrie, not a human. To her, meat's meat. One thing you can't do up here is ascribe human characteristics to animals. They have many of our same needs, but approach life without all our hang-ups."

Carrie shook her head. "I still can't believe I'm living with a man who could do something like that." Bart started to say something, but she interrupted him. "If I decide I want to leave, you promise you'll get me out of here? No matter what?"

"I'll do my best."

"That's not good enough. Promise you'll get me out of here."

Bart shrugged. "I promise I'll do my best."

CARRIE LEARNED that living in her new home, whether it be for a day or a week or a month or a year, was about survival; nothing more. Her choices were the choices of necessity and there was no way she could survive, let alone escape, without Bart's help. When he taught her about his homestead and the wilderness, she listened intently to what he had to say and thought he was an excellent teacher, if nothing else.

And she watched as well as listened. She studied the way Bart sawed and split wood for the fires, how he cut the thinner branches for kindling, how he set the wood stove, what his technique was for lighting the Coleman lanterns without breaking their mantles. She joined him in his struggle to keep a section of the small stream that flowed near the cabin from freezing by chopping open the ice several times a day so they would always have fresh water. She brushed snow from the top rows of the woodpiles and carried armfuls of logs and kindling into the cabin. She made the bed every morning and swept the floor with the goose wing every afternoon and took over cooking and disposing of their refuse in a slop hole deep in the woods. While these activities were foreign to her life in La Jolla, they had a certain logic that intrigued her, and the more she did, the better she felt about herself for she hoped that she was making contributions—as small as they may be—to her survival. It was the first time in her life she felt that she was gaining control.

ON HER FOURTH DAY, Carrie stood at the wood-stove cooking breakfast, the smell of corned beef hash filling the cabin. She had rolled the sleeves of Bart's black-and-white-checked wool shirt to her elbows and was singing *Whatever Lola Wants, Lola Gets.* She turned to set two forks and two strips from a roll of paper towels on the card table, absentmindedly clearing the book Bart had been reading from the table and tossing it on his pillow. It landed title side up and Carrie made a small noise as though the wind had been knocked from her. *In The Lake Of The Woods?* Why was he reading that, of all books? She picked up the book and opened it to the page he'd turned down to mark where he finished reading. A thin pencil line was drawn opposite two paragraphs. She glanced out the window to see if he was nearby, and hurriedly began to read:

"Multiple calamities had come to mind. A bad fall. Lacerations, broken bones. Kathy was smart, yes, but she didn't know shit about this wilderness. A suburb slicker. That was the joke between them: how she adored nature but didn't see why it had to be outside. Opposites were built into her personality. Contradiction was the rule. She enjoyed her morning stroll, the solitude and fresh air, but even then she conceived of nature as a department store with potted trees and a gigantic glass roof.

Which could turn unfortunate."

"Which could turn unfortunate?" she blurted out. "Oh, my God." Was he planning on getting rid of her if she didn't work out? She drew a deep breath and set the book by the stove and finished preparing breakfast. She would get her answers soon.

A moment later Bart clumped into the cabin, followed by Lola. He set an armful of firewood in the dwindling stack by the stove and hung his parka on a peg by the door. He reached for his coffee cup and sat at the table and looked at Carrie over the brim of his cup as he took a drink. "There's something we should talk about."

"There sure is," Carrie said. She shoved a plate of hash in front of him and picked up the book and waved at him. "What's this all about?"

Bart shrugged. "It's about a guy who loses a senate race—"

"That's not what I'm asking." She opened the book to the marked page and tapped it hard with her finger. "How come you marked this part of the book? Does it have to do with me? What could turn unfortunate? What have you—"

Bart put his hands up in mock surrender. "Whoa, Carrie! What's going on here? That's what I wanted to talk to you about."

"You tell me what's going on," she stammered. "Are you planning on killing me the way you did the dogs?"

Bart chuckled and looked up at her and smiled. "Just the opposite. This passage reminded me that we should do everything we can so things *don't* turn unfortunate." He took the book from her and set it on the table. "I think it's time you learned to shoot the carbine so you can prevent any calamities that might come your way, or if anything should happen to me."

"That's it? That's truly it?"

"That's truly it, Carrie. Right now it seems you're tilting at windmills. Sooner or later you've got to trust me."

She thought maybe Bart was right. Maybe she was a bit on edge. But who wouldn't be? She set her breakfast on the table and sat. "I'm not a violent person. Just the thought of learning to shoot makes me feel like the Unabomber. Violence is what …" She was about to say, what she didn't like about Jake Hornbeck, but stopped. "Violence is what I hated about the thing with the dogs; what it says about you; that you're capable of such a thing."

"I understand, but out here you've got to think ahead. Knowing how to shoot a rifle doesn't mean you're a violent person. No matter what you think, I don't consider myself violent but if anything should ever happen to me—if there's ever an emergency—you should know how to shoot, and shoot well."

What was he trying to tell her? To turn her into? Why did he keep talking about harm? Emergencies? Nonetheless, she reasoned, she should know how to protect herself in case she was attacked by a bear or something for someday it might come in handy.

And so, on that sunny, cloudless October morning, Carrie began to add shooting a rifle to her growing arsenal of survival skills. She and Bart, faithfully followed by Lola, snowshoed to the edge of the meadow where Bart brushed snow from a tree stump and set an empty tin can on it. He led Carrie several yards away and wrapped his arms around her and nestled the butt of the rifle against her shoulder. It was the first time Bart had embraced her since she'd arrived in the wilderness and she was comforted by his touch and surprised at how much she'd missed it.

"Someday this might be important," he said. "Maybe even the difference between life and death." He turned her toward the target and lowered the rifle into her hands. "Don't worry, it's not loaded. Just practice breathing easily to center yourself. Then cock it, like this." He worked the rifle's lever. "Aim carefully and slowly squeeze the trigger." Still holding the rifle in her hands he pointed it in the direction of the can and pulled the trigger. The hammer fell with a metallic click. "See? It's really pretty simple." He worked the rifle's lever again and repeated his instructions. "Just remember: cock, aim and squeeze. Cock, aim and squeeze."

Once she was convinced that she understood what she was supposed to do, she asked if she could shoot a real bullet.

"You're ready?"

She thought the last time Bart had asked if she was ready she was sitting in the dog sled freezing her butt off about to start her trip into the wilderness with absolutely no idea what she was committing to. Compared to that, shooting the rifle had to be a piece of cake. "Ready," she said, "but only to learn. Not to do any killing or anything."

"I understand," Bart said, and took a cartridge from the pocket of his jacket. "Now watch." He wrapped his arms around her again. "You push the bullet in here." He inserted the cartridge in the carbine's loading port. "Then you work the lever and that puts the cartridge in the chamber." He pushed the lever down and back and lowered the hammer with his thumb. "Putting the hammer down makes the rifle safe, even when it's got a bullet in the chamber. Okay?"

Carrie nodded.

"*Now* you're good to go. Remember: take a deep breath, then pull back the hammer, aim and squeeze." He let go of her and stepped aside.

She cocked the rifle, pointed it in the general direction of the can, closed her eyes tight and jerked on the trigger. The rifle's recoil pushed her off balance and for an instant she teetered with one snowshoe caught over the other and then fell on her butt deep in the snow. "Wow! Did I hit it? Well, did I?"

Bart reached for her hand and pulled her to her feet. He smiled and shook his head. "You need a bit more practice. You missed it by a mile."

"Can I try it again? I want to do it right."

"After you've done a little more dry firing," Bart said.

"A little what?"

"Practicing without bullets." He took the carbine from her and ejected the spent casing. "We need to save as many bullets as we can."

Something told her that Bart was right: she should learn, just in case. In case of what, she wasn't sure, but she was committed to succeeding for once in her life. "Okay. I'll work on this," she said. "I can do it. I know I can."

"I know you can, too," Bart said. "I've known ever since I met you that you can do anything you put your mind to."

As they started to snowshoe back to the cabin Carrie noticed a red spot in the snow where the sled dog had been sitting. She grabbed Bart's sleeve and pointed. "Look. Lola's bleeding."

"She must be coming into heat."

"Well, good for her," Carrie said. "I'd love to see her become a mom."

Bart laughed. "Not much chance of that."

Carrie thought, especially since he'd killed all the other dogs and was feeding them to Lola. And then she scolded herself. No more of that. He had to do it, and she had to get over it.

7

I N THE DAYS THAT FOLLOWED Carrie snowshoed
through the woods, practicing dry firing the rifle, working its lever to cock it, aligning the sights on imaginary tar-
gets—a small evergreen bow drooping heavily with snow,
the wounded stump of a fractured sapling—then squeezing
the trigger until the hammer fell. Soon she convinced Bart
that she was ready to try live firing again and, after a couple
of practice sessions, could hit a can at fifty yards, two out of
three times. At the end of the last session, Bart called her
"a regular Annie Oakley." Carrie smiled at him, not as much
for the compliment but because she was beginning to realize
that the more she learned, the more capable a survivor she
became and the less trapped she felt and the better she felt
about herself. And about Bart.

The last day of the week that she'd promised she'd stay—
she guessed it was the last day, it was difficult to be sure what
day it was without a radio or a newspaper, let alone a TV—
Carrie finished her lunch and bundled into her down parka
anxious to capture what was left of the afternoon sunlight.
Once outside she took her snowshoes from their pegs and
called for Lola. She'd grown to enjoy their outings together,
the sled dog loping playfully through the snow following her

everywhere she went, and was anxious to have her company. Her snowshoes fastened, she clapped her mittened hands and called again. She waited a moment and clapped and whistled. "Come on, Lola! Let's go. It's girly time!" She waited another moment. When the husky didn't appear Carrie thought she must be with her master who was deep in the forest cutting firewood and, comfortable that all was well, set out toward the meadow on her own.

On her first explorations with Bart, Carrie had been surprised at the exhilarating feeling of being out in the cold for she had dreaded it and was confused by what she had felt. The crunching of the snow beneath the webs of her snowshoes and the feel of the sun mixed with the cold air on her face pleased her and she had quickly found an easy rhythm to her snowshoeing that settled her into a relaxed, happy state, much like the trance she experienced while swimming endless laps in college—but without the pressure of performance. And, on those early trips, as Bart and she snowshoed farther and farther from the cabin, he pointed out the animal tracks in the freshly fallen snow, the tracks of the wolf, the fox, lynx, deer and moose, and she had asked, "Where are the bears?"

"This time of year, they're hibernating," Bart answered and instantly Carrie felt embarrassed.

"Damn," she muttered, and put her question right up there with bringing her blow dryer and cell phone and her *Paradise Found* undies, although she had to admit that she was getting closer every night to pulling those panties from her duffle and modeling them for Bart.

As she snowshoed, the shadow of the raven darkened the snow in front of her and she smiled and saluted as it set its wings and glided to a tree at the edge of the woods. Her calm, welcoming reaction to the large black bird that had once frightened her made her think how proud Hannah would be of her, and with the thought of Hannah she realized that her time was up, that she had to make *the* critical decision—stay or go—when she caught sight of a dark form at the foot of the trees that bordered the open field.

She stopped for a moment, suddenly afraid, but then thought she had nothing to fear for, as she had learned—the hard way—the grizzlies were in hibernation. She told herself to be calm and wondered if she'd surprised a young moose or caribou and pushed her dark glasses on top of her wool cap to get a better look. Squinting to see into the shadows of the trees, she heard the faint rustle of branches and the flap of wings and looked over her shoulder as the raven took flight, jabbering as it climbed above her and then dove directly for her. She ducked and closed her eyes and felt the tips of the raven's wings brush her face as he plucked her sunglasses from her cap. Bart had told her stories of these mischievous birds stealing clothes pins from laundry lines and pulling the tails of sleeping dogs, but, up until now, Carrie had thought these yarns were just part of the Alaska wilderness lore.

"Hey, come back with those!" she screamed and turned to follow the bird's flight. The raven pumped his wings for a moment and then banked slowly, flapped his wings to a stall and opened his thick beak and let the sunglasses fall to Carrie's feet. She dug through the snow until she found them, stood and brushed the snow from them, all the while watching the raven as he disappeared into the distance. "What's with you?" she called. "Are you trying to tell me something?"

She looked again at the dark form at the edge of the woods, now more curious than concerned. Soon she realized what she was witnessing: Lola was tangled with another animal. They turned in the fading sunlight and she saw what she thought was a large dark dog humping her husky. She snowshoed toward them as fast as she could, screaming, "Get away from her, you bastard! Let my little girl alone!" but by the time she reached the dogs, they were turned butt to butt, locked tight in a copulatory tie.

Carrie stopped no more than ten yards from the animals and, as she did, the male curled back his long black lips and snarled.

Good God, she thought, it's a wolf!

Her first reaction was to turn and run, but she stood in place and looked at the wolf for he was the most gorgeous animal she'd ever seen. His thick coat was black and brown and his large slanted eyes a gem-like yellow. Still locked with Lola, the wolf lowered his shoulders and his ears and stretched his forelegs before him, a circular scar on his ankle showing above the tamped snow. He drew his lips back and showed his huge incisors and growled again and Carrie finally realized that she was standing—unarmed—near an animal that once free from Lola could kill her in an instant.

She began to back away, never taking her eyes from the wolf, thinking how stupid she was not to carry the rifle when she was out on her own, and swore she'd never make that mistake again. When she'd traveled a hundred yards, the dog and the wolf separated and Carrie could feel her heart racing even faster, for now there was nothing to stop the wolf from attacking her. She stood motionless, trying not to excite him.

The wolf continued to stare at her, then lowered his head and laid his ears back. His look filled her with fear and then she heard him growl, and she thought, this was it. Eaten by a wolf just when her life might be turning around. Who would ever believe it? Maybe she should just walk away and hope for the best. That way, at least, she wouldn't see him coming. But, before she could move, Lola began porpoising through the snow, her tail wagging eagerly until she reached Carrie and pushed her head between her legs. Still keeping her eyes on the wolf, Carrie reached down and rubbed a mitten over Lola's ears. The wolf cocked his head and watched for a moment and then rolled on his back and began licking his bright pink penis that looked so out of place in the cold and the snow and the woods that Carrie couldn't help but laugh. She chucked the dog's ears once more and asked, "Was he good? Was that fun?" and headed back to the cabin, hoping the wolf had more important things on his mind than attacking her. Lola followed at her side as though she were protecting her. In turn, Carrie talked to her in loud, bold tones, her nerves still very much on edge. When she finally got up the courage to see if the wolf was following them, he was nowhere to be seen. She let out a sigh of relief. "Okeydokey," she said. "So that's what Bart calls 'living on the edge.'" For a place that Hannah said would bore her to tears, there never seemed to be a dull moment. That was thrilling, she thought, but what if Lola was pregnant? Would Bart kill her, too? Or just her pups? She couldn't let either happen. She let out a heavy sigh. "Whatever. It's our secret—at least for now, until we see what happens—but you're a naughty, naughty girl." Carrie smiled for she only half meant it; there was no reason that Lola should be deprived of one of life's great pleasures just because she was stranded in the middle of nowhere, in the middle of winter.

"And," she wondered aloud, "why should I?"

WITH DARKNESS SETTLING around her, Carrie returned to the warmth and protection of the small cabin, a place she now thought of as a tiny boat in the middle of a frigid ocean, but a boat sturdy enough to withstand any storm. While she waited for Bart to return from working in the woods, she fed Lola and again worried about what Bart would do if she were pregnant. She thought she'd cross that bridge when they came to it—if she were still around to protect her dog—and began to prepare their evening meal and wrestle with the more immediate, all-encompassing question and scolded herself to remain objective and realistic.

Was Bart the man to spend the winter with? The man for her? Throughout the week she had become convinced that he was; he was so patient and gentle and understanding, and damned good-looking, too. But hadn't she gotten so many men wrong so many times before? And, again, she wondered once more how well she really knew him. He not only killed the dogs but he seemed to be running from something, although she wasn't sure what. But wasn't she running from something, too?

She tried to weigh the life that lay ahead of her. She liked the newness and the simplicity and privacy and the adventure of it all, although she wondered if she'd ever truly grow accustomed to wearing long johns and wool socks every moment of every day. And, while she was learning to deal with the cold, what about the "damned darkness?" What would that really be like? Was there no way to tell but to experience it?

All good questions, she thought. All without good answers.

She didn't raise the subject at supper—nor did she talk about Lola and her encounter with the wolf—and Bart seemed to purposefully avoid the topic and she decided to wait to discuss it until she'd had one more night to sleep on it.

After they finished eating, she braved taking her first bath since arriving. She stepped into the darkness and pushed toward the sauna through the swirling, wind-driven snow that had drifted well up the cabin's log walls. Inside, she lit the Coleman lantern and the woodstove. While waiting for the hard-packed snow and icicles to melt and warm in the galvanized tub she had placed on the stove, she held the lantern above the hand mirror that hung from the wall and took a long look at herself. In the dim light she could see she was still tanned, but thought that wouldn't last much longer in the cold and the dark. She ran a hand through her curls to loosen them and thought she could use a little sprucing up.

The cramped sauna warmed quickly and Carrie dipped the warmed water from the tub with a white enamel pitcher and poured it over her shoulders, enjoying the water's warmth as it ran over and down her before disappearing through the slats in the floor. She washed her hair and then her underclothes and thought, not quite her shower in La Jolla, but warm all the same, and it made her feel fresh. When she was finished drying herself, she lathered her face with Dermatone, something Bart had encouraged her to do to protect her skin from frostnip and wind burn. She put on lipstick, deodorant and her *Paradise Found* undies and pulled on her ski pants, her socks and heavy boots and zipped her down jacket over her bare breasts. She took a look in the mirror, thought, not too bad, and collected her wet undies, long johns and sweater and sprinted to the main cabin, her wet curls and eyelashes frozen stiff before she reached the cabin door.

She entered the warm cabin surrounded by an envelope of frigid air. Bart was sitting in bed, reading Robert Service's poetry, his faded red long johns unbuttoned to the middle of his chest. He closed his book and flipped the blankets back, inviting her to join him as she hung her wet bra and panties on the nails that supported the rifle above the woodstove.

She slipped off her boots and placed them side by side with Bart's and unzipped her down parka and could feel his eyes follow the zipper to her breasts where they stopped. "Oh," she said. Strip tease, wilderness style. Well? Well, why not? What harm can come from it? It wasn't as though she was making a commitment or anything. She smiled and pulled her arms slowly from their sleeves, then hung the parka on its peg by the door. She turned and wiggled her ski pants down her butt and legs to her ankles and stepped out of them. Stretching to her tiptoes, she hung her pants by their suspenders over her parka and brushed snow away from their legs, and then shuffled her sock-clad feet toward Bart as slowly as her pounding heart would let her. *Paradise Found* on her undies now seemed okay. Maybe even better than okay.

She lay on top of Bart and pulled the blankets over them. He wrapped his arms around her and held her tight against him. "Welcome back," he said. "Welcome home. I hope you'll stay." He held her for a long while without speaking.

The warmth of his body was comforting and his silence peaceful and somehow reassuring and she felt her cares and worries fall away.

Moments passed. Neither spoke nor moved. Carrie felt herself settle and then Bart slid his hand over her buttocks. "Paradise found?"

"Not quite," she whispered, "but we may be heading in the right direction."

"What can I do—?" Bart asked, but before he could finish his question, Carrie's kiss silenced him.

There was no rush to decide. Certainly not at that moment, she thought, as she felt them become one. All that complicated stuff could wait until morning.

Bart began to move beneath her.

"Oh," she whispered.

What the hell, why shouldn't she give it a few more days?

She pushed up from the bed and arched her back and muttered, "Oh," again and looked down at Bart and smiled. "Oh, my God!" she grunted and kissed him deeply as every tense fiber of her body relaxed at once. As she began to calm, she thought, for better or for worse, Bart had won. She was with him until the breakup and hoped she'd made the right choice for once because, if she hadn't, there was no turning back.

8

IN THE WEEKS that followed Carrie's decision, the Alaska wilderness tightened its grip. The window of daylight narrowed. The snow deepened and drifted closer to the cabins' roofs. The temperature dropped to zero and Bart and she became focused on the chores that Carrie now accepted as those that had to be completed to survive. All took time, and she and Bart worked hard to find the quickest, most efficient way to deal with each. Once they'd worked out a routine, all their duties—large and small—were done every day in the same order and the same manner, all with a quiet sense of dependency and good-humored understanding.

Bringing dry firewood to the cabin and cutting, splitting and storing wood was part of almost every day's routine. Bart called it "Job One," and had said, "The goal's to keep the cabin somewhere between forty and fifty degrees, and that'll take at least sixty cords to survive the winter."

"Forty degrees? Indoors?" Carrie said. "Bart, I'm from southern California, remember? I'm a warm-weather girl. Beaches, bikinis, stuff like that. I'll freeze to death at forty degrees."

Bart smiled. "We'll work down to it gradually. You'll get used to it in no time. Besides, you're a lot tougher than you think."

"You're sure?"

"I'm sure."

While she hoped Bart was right, every night before going to bed Carrie banked the woodstove and left the damper slightly open and, throughout the night, reset the fire to keep the temperature from dropping too low. Make the best of it, she told herself. There was no reason why, with a little extra work, she couldn't see this adventure through in comfort.

When they weren't doing chores or weren't imprisoned by whiteouts or howling gales that shook the cabin walls, they snowshoed through the woods and the meadows, followed by Lola who had to work hard to keep up in the deep snow. During these outings Carrie enjoyed a sense of freedom that she'd never felt before and marveled at the beauty of all that was about her: the snow-laden hemlocks, the vast, white open spaces, and the mountains—especially the towering, flat-topped Mt. Logan that changed its colors throughout the day, a process that Carrie thought matched her many moods. And, in the early afternoons, as the blackness descended on them once again, Bart would read poetry aloud while Carrie cooked their supper. Robert Service's "The Cremation of Sam McGee" became her favorite poem and, in time, she could recite it from memory:

> There are strange things done in the midnight sun
> By the men who moil for gold;
> The Arctic trails have their secret tales
> That would make your blood run cold;
> The Northern Lights have seen queer sights…

Many evenings, in search of those Northern Lights, Bart and she would snowshoe to the meadow, their path made clear by the light of the moon. It was there that Bart would teach her about the stars and their constellations. Those were the best nights Carrie could have ever imagined. When they returned to the light and warmth of their cabin they'd crawl under their heavy blankets and talk and keep their bodies close together as though they were the last two people on earth and, at times, Carrie fantasized that they were.

When they were ready to call it a day, as they drifted off to sleep, Carrie would listen to the distant cry of the wolf and would try to imagine him in her mind, so beautiful, so wild, his howl now a comforting sound, yet a call that she secretly was convinced was for Lola who lay curled in her dog house just outside the door at the end of the heavy chain that kept her from roaming, from visiting her secret boyfriend.

SEVERAL WEEKS after Carrie had found Lola locked with the wolf, Bart and she lay in bed waiting for the cabin to warm before they started their breakfast. He put his hand under her nightgown and she rolled toward him, eventually sitting upright on him, grabbing her curls tight with both hands and grinding Bart in big, slow circles, thinking not having to worry about anyone hearing her groanings or moanings— not Hannah, not Franny Jenoff, their nosey apartment super- intendent, not anyone—was one of the benefits of making love in the wilderness. But as she felt an explosion of tingling deep within her, she thought she heard a woman's voice and stopped moving to listen.

She heard the voice again. "Halloo the house."

"Oh, for Pete's sake!" Bart said. "It's Feather." As he spoke, Carrie could feel him lose interest in her and slowly pull from under her.

"Feather?" Carrie said. She crawled around on the bed, frantically trying to find her nightgown. "What are you talking about?" She turned in circles on the bed, naked except for her wool-socked feet. "*Who* are you talking about? I thought we were all alone."

Bart hurried into his long johns and pulled on his socks and the fleece pants he'd worn every day since they'd arrived. "We are," he said, "except for Feather. She kind of roams around."

"But you promised there'd be no more surprises." Before Bart could answer, there was a tapping on the window and Carrie turned to look but all she could see was two fur mittens cupped around a pair of wide-set dark eyes and a brown nose that was pressed flat against the glass.

Bart reached for the door and Carrie crawled beneath the covers and pulled them tight against her throat. Lying there, waiting to meet this unwanted intruder, she could still imagine Bart in her and wanted him back in bed and wanted the wilderness back to herself. This was her cabin, her small part of the wild, her new life, and she didn't want to share it with anyone but Bart and Lola.

When Bart pushed the door open and invited the woman in, instantly everything Carrie had begun to love changed. She was surprised at how much this interruption annoyed her and wondered if she was falling in love with her surroundings. Or with Bart. Or both.

She watched the stranger kick out of a pair of skis and slip a pack from her shoulders into the snow. The pack was almost as big as she was and in the dark Carrie could make out a rifle strapped across the top of it. Bart unlatched Lola's chain and suddenly the cabin felt very crowded as Bart, the intruder, and the sled dog stood by the woodstove as if they were posing for a group photograph, all looking at Carrie lying in bed, moving her hands underneath the covers in what she hoped were inconspicuous circles as she continued to try to find her nightgown.

At first, no one said a word. Bart stood still and shrugged and smiled at Carrie. The woman beside him, even in her heavy caribou pelt mukluks, was no taller than five feet. She stared at Carrie for a moment and then pulled off a rabbit's fur hat that covered her thick black pigtails and unzipped her puffy, quilted red parka. She stood like a little general inspecting her troops and while she wasn't what Carrie would call pretty—her face was too broad—she was handsome in a feminine and honest-looking way.

"Carrie, this is Feather," Bart said. "Feather, say hello to Carrie."

"That was quite a show," Feather said. "You're in a class by yourself."

"You watched?" Carrie asked.

"Up here, you take what you can get. Right, Bart? And you celebrate the temporary." She smiled at Carrie and, except for a missing upper canine that Carrie thought should be attended to immediately, she had a reassuring smile. "I especially liked the way you spun your nightshirt like a lasso when you got on top of lover boy, here."

Oh shit, Carrie thought. She'd forgotten about that part.

Feather bent over and picked Carrie's nightgown from beneath the table. "And I like that tattoo of yours. It's color-ful." She handed her nightgown to her. "Slip it on under the covers if you want. I've seen all I need to see."

Carrie did exactly as Feather suggested, at first feeling trapped beneath the covers and on the receiving end of a joke, but, while this small woman had a presence far larger than her physical stature, her body language seemed to signal that she was a friend, perhaps even a soul mate.

"What brings you out here?" Bart said. It was only one of about a hundred questions Carrie wanted to ask this intruder—and Bart.

"I dropped in on the Wrangell Mountain Lodge a couple of weeks ago and Whitey said you should be expecting company. He asked me to tell you that some guy from California left a message at the relay in Anchorage; he wants to come see you."

"Out here?" Carrie said. "To see us?"

"Yup," Feather said. "A Bill Davies or Davis. Whitey wasn't sure which. The transmission was kind of garbled."

What was going on? Carrie wondered. Only Hannah and her mom knew where she was. The whole idea was to be alone and now Bart and she had someone else in their home who said there may be others. Carrie didn't get it and didn't like it. She looked at Bart who he seemed as confused as she was. For the first time since she'd known him, he looked perplexed. "I don't know anyone named Davies or Davis," she said. "Do you?"

Bart shook his head and said maybe Whitey had things a bit mixed up, that no one in their right mind would try to come out here until after the breakup. "Except you, Feather." He smiled. "Anybody want some breakfast?"

Carrie got out of bed and pulled her cold-weather gear on over her nightgown and said, "*You* start breakfast, *lover boy*; I've got to pee."

As Carrie started for the door, Feather said, "One other thing. Whitey said to tell you that your roommate called Anchorage to say there'd been a murder in your apartment but that she was okay."

"Hannah called? A murder in my apartment?"

"Whitey didn't give a name," Feather said. "Only that your friend was okay, that someone had killed the person who manages your building."

"Mrs. Jenoff? Why ..." She was about to say she had been thinking about Mrs. Jenoff just moments ago when she was on top of Bart but stopped.

"Whitey most probably meant your apartment building," Bart said. "Hannah wouldn't be okay if there'd been a murder in your apartment."

Carrie felt relieved. He was right, it had to have been in the apartment building, but it must have been horrible, just the same. She asked Feather if that was all Whitey told her.

"That's all."

Carrie reached for the door and then asked, "Have they caught the murderer?"

Feather said Whitey didn't mention it if they had.

Bart lifted the skillet from the stove and turned it slowly in his hands. He looked at Carrie. "What's up?"

"Nothing," she said. "Just curious, that's all."

"You're sure?"

"I'm sure," she answered, although something told her that Jake may have taken a part in this but she wondered how he could he have known how to reach her unless ...

"You're not a very good liar, are you?" Feather asked.

"Yes. Well, no. I mean, yes, you're right," Carrie said. "I'm a bit shaken by your news, that's all." She stood for a moment without speaking, then forced a smile and excused herself to pee.

AFTER BREAKFAST Carrie sat on the edge of the bed and sipped a cup of coffee and began to ask Feather a string of questions. She had none for Bart, at least not at that moment; those would have to wait until Feather left.

"Been here all my life," Feather said. "Born near Gulkana. You know where that is? Up near the Copper?"

Carrie looked at Bart. "The Copper's one of the rivers we flew over, right?"

Bart nodded but seemed to be somewhere else.

"I'm an Ahtna widow," Feather continued. "My husband was killed when I was nineteen. Mauled by a grizzly. Been on my own ever since and I kind of like it that way. I carry everything I own on my back and ski or walk anywhere and everywhere I need to go. I may not look it, but I'm strong like an ox. Never met a man I couldn't out-ski or out-fish or out-shoot. Right, Bart?"

"Absolutely." From the look in Bart's eyes and the manner in which he said it, Carrie knew he meant it and felt a flash of jealousy.

"But I can't do all the stuff in bed that you do," Feather said and turned to Bart. "Right?"

Bart got up from the table and poured himself another cup as though nothing at all had been said while Carrie tried to stay calm. She folded her hands in her lap and raised her eyebrows and said, "I take it Bart and you have spent some time together." And then added with a feigned smile, "How nice."

"Hasn't he told you?" Feather said.

"I guess he did." Carrie nodded and smiled at Bart—the son of a bitch who was going to have a freezing goddamn no nookie winter trying to talk his way out of this. "Why, yes, I guess he did," she said again and laughed a little laugh. "It must have slipped my mind, mustn't it have, Bart?"

"Sorry. I wasn't paying attention." He looked uncomfortable for the first time since Carrie had met him. Even when he'd been challenged by Jake he'd been calm and cool. He asked how Feather's brother was doing and Carrie thought it was a clumsy attempt to change the subject; that she was learning all sorts of things about Bart this morning, that he *could* worry about things and *couldn't* manage everything to perfection.

"Storyteller?" Feather said. "He's doing just fine. Says he's got some new ones I'd never believe."

"Storyteller? That's your brother's name?" Carrie asked.

"He tells a lot of tall stories," Feather said. "Like all my people, I used to think he made them up, but now I don't think he does. He's always been an honest kid and swears he's telling the truth. So, I take him at his word."

"I've always thought they were true," Bart said. "There's something special about him. Hopefully, Carrie, you'll get a chance to see for yourself. The last few years he's visited every spring." He took a sip of his coffee and asked Feather where she was headed.

"Up to Bremner. I'm going to winter at the old mine."

Bart told her that she was welcome to stay with them for a few days, if she'd like.

"Bart," Carrie said, a slight scolding tone in her voice, "where would she sleep?"

Feather tapped Carrie on the arm. "Don't worry, sister. I'm moving west." She looked at Bart. "Can you spare a handful of bullets for the carbine?"

Bart took a half-full box of Winchester 30-30 ammunition from the shelf by the stove and handed it to her. "That enough?"

"Plenty," she said and winked at Carrie. "I *never* miss." She stood and shook Carrie's hand and said it was nice to meet her and wished her good luck. "I'll check in on you in the spring."

"That would be nice," Carrie said. She was surprised by her words but meant what she said.

Feather smiled. "And don't worry, I won't hang around. It's the way we look after one another up here." She hugged Bart good-bye, stepped over the sled dog to get to the door and asked what they called their dog.

Bart looked away. "Lola."

Feather gave Bart a disdainful look and laughed. "Lola, the grizzly queen. No one's seen hide nor hair of her since the breakup."

"I think she went back east," Bart said.

"She take her bear traps with her?" Feather laughed again and turned to Carrie and said, "You're feeding your husky too much." She winked as though she and Carrie knew something Bart didn't and without another word pushed the door open and slipped out into the low morning sun.

9

BART PICKED UP HIS CUP and stood but Carrie raised a hand to hold him in place. "You stay put, *lover boy*. I'll get it." She poured him his coffee and stood over him, her arms folded tight across her fleece. She tapped the toe of her boot on the caribou skin that covered the floor. "Okay, let's hear it."

Bart gave her a confused look. "Hear what?"

He appeared puzzled, and Carrie shook her head in disbelief. Either he was a great actor or thick as a plank. Maybe it was because he'd never seen her mad as hell before. She had so many questions she didn't know where to begin. She tapped her foot again. "Let's start with Feather."

"What about her?"

"Why didn't you tell me about her?"

"You never asked."

Carrie raised her eyebrows and looked at the ceiling. Good Lord. Bart's law: if she didn't ask, he didn't tell. "You *can* volunteer things, you know. Not every conversation has to be an Easter egg hunt. We've got time—all the time in the world as a matter of fact—to talk about anything and everything. I want to know about people like Feather. I want to know about you. *All* about you."

Bart stared at his coffee cup as he pushed it in a circle on the table. "Feather spent a winter here."

"Just one?"

Bart nodded slowly but didn't look up. "Two winters ago."

"What about last winter and the winters before her?"

Bart didn't answer, just continued to move his cup about the table.

"I assume that means there were others."

"You sound surprised." He seemed annoyed. "I never told you that you were the first."

Because she'd never asked.

"Was Lola one of them?"

Bart nodded and laughed in the same disdainful manner that Feather had. "She didn't work out. She was paranoid about grizzlies and had Whitey fly in a bunch of bear traps before she'd agree to come. The damn things weighed a ton."

"But you named my dog after her."

"We can change it if you'd like."

Carrie looked down at Lola who looked up at her and banged her tail on the floor. "No. I like it. It fits her." She tried to put her thoughts in order. One step at a time, she told herself. First things first. She cleared her throat. "Okay," she said, addressing herself as much as Bart, "let's stick with Feather. How did you two get along?"

"If Feather's your friend, she's the best friend you'll ever have."

"So she was your friend?"

Again Bart nodded without looking up. "She still is."

Carrie felt her heart begin to race. "Nothing more?"

"Being a good friend's not enough?" Bart said.

"Sure it is," Carrie said. "But I was asking if you were…
you know…romantically involved."

Bart laughed. "Not on your life. We're too much alike.
Feather's as much a loner as I am."

Carrie was relieved by his answer but didn't like the way
he described himself. It was so exclusive of others. Of her.
"If you're such a loner, why Feather and the others? Why
me?"

"I told you before," Bart said softly. "Companionship's a
key to survival up here. You wouldn't want to try this on your
own. It would be very damn tough."

"But—"

He finally looked up. "If you're going to ask about the
others, don't because they weren't important. Feather became
a friend; the rest didn't."

Fine, she thought, but now what she really wanted to
know was, how was she working out? She was beginning
to wonder if she were anything more than a mechanism
for survival. She poured some coffee to give herself some
time to think. She thought Bart was telling the truth and
tried to accept Feather as nothing more than a friend; that
the others weren't worth worrying about. She pulled the
empty chair from the table and sat; she thought she'd put
off questioning Bart about their relationship, at least for
now. She took a deep breath, let it out slowly and her tone
softened. "I do have some other things that are bothering
me."

Bart said she should get them out on the table. "Once
and for all."

"Okay," she said. "Who is this guy Bill Davis, or Davies?"

"I was about to ask you."

"You mean you don't know? You're not keeping something from me?"

Bart shook his head. "Carrie, let's make a simple pact: no lies between us. Deal?"

"Deal."

Bart smiled, but the smile left his face quickly. "I haven't a clue who the guy might be." He fixed his soft, trusting gray eyes on hers. "And you?"

"Me neither," Carrie said, but the thought that it might be Jake Hornbeck flitted through her mind again.

"You're sure?"

"I'm sure," she answered, and felt guilty for not telling the whole truth.

"Good," Bart said. "Maybe they got the message garbled in Anchorage. The relay system to the lodge is kind of primitive. What's next?"

Carrie rocked in her chair. She wanted to understand and feel comfortable with his answers. Her words came slowly. "Why are you here? Really?"

"I've told you: for the adventure; to live on the edge."

His tone was a bit impatient. Carrie thought he was giving her his stock answer, and was surprised by her next question, not only by her matter-of-fact tone but because it was one she hadn't thought to ask before. "Is someone looking for *you*?"

"If you're asking if I'm wanted by the police or something like that, the answer is no." He laughed. "Just the opposite, actually. I don't think anyone in the whole world gives a damn where I am. What about you?"

"My mom and Hannah care."

"That's not what I'm asking. Is someone looking for *you?*"

"No," Carrie said. "I'm not hiding from anyone or anything."

"Not even that Hornbeck guy?"

"There's no way he could know how to find me."

"Could Hannah have told him?"

"Over her dead body," Carrie said. She stared at Bart who stared back at her. Both knew what the other was thinking but neither spoke. Lola looked up at them with her pale blue eyes, thumped her tail on the floor and lowered her head and let out a low grunting sound through her nose, and the cabin went silent.

"No!" Bart finally said. "No. It's okay. It's okay. We needn't worry about that. No one can find us here." He began to stand but Carrie placed a hand on his arm and settled him back in his chair.

"One more time," she said. "Why are you here? I know it's for the adventure, but why else? Please, talk to me. That's what this time together is all about."

"Oh, boy," Bart muttered. He straightened in his chair and stretched his arms above his head and sighed. "About six years ago I got crossways with the school where I was teaching and it kind of escalated until it seemed I was arguing about everything with the local school board. It wasn't quite McFee versus the Board of Education, but it came pretty damn close, and for a couple of months it seemed as though my name was in the newspapers almost every day. Finally, the school began talking about not wanting to renew my contract and..." he paused, "...and in the middle of it all, Polly asked for a divorce."

"That's the first time you've mentioned her name," Carrie said. She covered one of his hands with hers. "Sorry. Go on."

He looked down at the table. "I don't much like talking about this and I try to keep her out of it as much as possible."

"Do you still love her?"

"Polly?" He hesitated. "Not an easy question, but not anymore. It took one hell of a long time to get over her but she remarried last year and that was the end of it. It was kind of a signal that it was time for me to move on."

"One more question?"

He nodded, but Carrie sensed he was uncomfortable saying more. Even so, she thought it would be best to get it all out as Bart had suggested. "Why did she want a divorce? It couldn't have just been the school thing."

Bart said there was more. Carrie waited for him to continue. She looked about the cabin. Took a sip of her coffee. Undid the top snaps on her fleece. Listened to Lola groan and shift her position on the floor. Finally, she whispered, "Please, Bart, I'll understand."

"The issue was kids. Not whether or not we should have them, but why we couldn't. We blamed each other, but were both too stubborn to do the tests. Don't ask me why. I still can't explain it. I said I'd get tested if she would. She said I should go first. I told her it was a team effort. It got so neither one of us was willing to give an inch. It made me feel like I was fighting everything and everybody, and when Polly said she wanted a divorce I decided to make a clean break from it all, and here I am, hoping I've learned something."

"Has she gotten pregnant since she remarried?" Carrie said.

"Not that I know of."

"So the odds are fifty-fifty you're okay?"

"I guess."

She felt she'd taken the first step toward really understanding this man. "Thanks for all that, but…"

"But what?"

"Do you plan to stay here forever? Plan to die here without anyone knowing where you are or *who* you are? Without anyone caring?"

"I haven't really thought about it," he said, "but seeing that I don't have anyone to miss me now, why would anyone miss me in the future?"

"Maybe someone cares about you that you don't even know about."

"I doubt it," Bart said. "I don't have any family left. My Dad died of a heart attack when I was six. My Mom was killed in a car crash ten years later and my sister died of ovarian cancer at thirty-two. I'm not a fatalist but, because of all that, I only live for the present." He paused. "But, not to worry, time heals all wounds. Well, almost all."

Carrie leaned toward him and kissed him lightly on the lips. "I'm sorry, and I'm sorry about all these questions, too, but I have one more." She wanted to ask where she fit in the scheme of things, but she didn't, and for the first time since the morning had begun she smiled. "Do you agree with Feather about how well I…you know…how good I am in bed?"

"Absolutely."

"But is that all I'm good for?" Carrie said.

"Far from it."

"You're serious?"

"Absolutely."

Carrie was elated by his answer and thought that her questioning had gone far enough. At least for now. Suddenly she wanted to finish what they had started before Feather had interrupted them. She stripped off her fleece, pulled her nightie over her head, stepped onto her chair and wrapped her legs around Bart's waist and her arms around his neck. "Be advised," she whispered, "the best is yet to come."

She pressed her forehead against his and stared into his amused eyes, the eyes that when she had first met him had seemed so filled with dreams. Maybe now they would all come true; for once it seemed they just might. For a moment she didn't move or speak. There were so many things that had become clear this morning and so many more that she didn't understand:

Bart's friend Feather and a boy named Storyteller.

A murder in her apartment building.

A stranger named Bill Davies or Bill Davis.

A pregnant sled dog.

And Bart.

And what they meant to each other.

10

AFTER FEATHER'S VISIT Bart and Carrie went back to their routine, adjusting to temperatures that hovered around zero during the twilight days of the impending darkness and then dropped to ten below, or lower, at night. "But," Bart assured her as he knelt in front of the woodstove, "as long as we keep ahead of our chores, we'll be ready for anything." He gave her a pained smile and massaged the side of his jaw with his fingertips. "Except maybe this." He winced slightly. "You know what this camp needs?"

"A flush toilet?" Carrie said. "I think I've got frostbite on my butt."

"Good guess, but no."

"I know, electricity!"

"Nope."

"How about running water, like for a shower and washing the dishes and our dirty clothes?"

Bart winced and raked his fingers down the side of his jaw. "Wrong again."

"A phone line?"

He shook his head and grimaced.

"Are you okay?" Carrie asked.

"I'm fine," he said. "What else?"

She guessed a gas stove.

Bart poked at the embers. "Not a bad idea, but not what I had in mind." His speech was slow and thick.

"Bart, look at me." She held his face and gently lifted it toward her. "What's the matter?"

"I've got a bit of a toothache, that's all."

"A bit of a toothache?"

"I'll be fine," he said and asked if she had any more guesses.

"Let's see. Electricity, plumbing, sanitation, food preparation and communications are all out."

"Right, and you're doing great without them."

His comment made Carrie forget for a moment that he was in pain. It reminded her of the lecture Hannah had given her before she left that had almost made her change her mind at the last minute. But now, Hannah's comments didn't bother her at all. Quite the contrary. She was proud of herself for not having changed her mind; for not having given in. She had survived without any of the amenities that Hannah had said she couldn't live without, and now she felt superior to people who couldn't do without them even though she thought it would be nice to have a hospital nearby, again as Hannah had said, in case she or Bart got sick or got mauled by a bear. But Bart and she were in the pink of health and it was winter—serious winter—and the bears were hibernating, so all was okay.

"What else could there possibly be?" she asked.

Bart latched the stove's heavy iron door and stood. "A totem pole."

Carrie blinked and stared wide-eyed at him. "Of course," she said and giggled. "A totem pole."

"Right," Bart said. "Every camp should have one."

"Silly me. Of course, a totem pole," Carrie said again. "Why didn't I think of that?"

Bart pulled a small pad of paper and a ballpoint pen from the shallow drawer in the table, and sat and began to draw. "Look. It would be our totem, our guardian."

Oh, my God, he's serious, she thought, but liked the way he said "*Our* totem, *our* guardian." She covered his hand with hers. "Did you and the others have one?"

Bart grimaced. "Nope." He dropped the pen and placed his hands on either side of his jaw. "This thing's beginning to hurt like hell."

"Have you taken any aspirin?"

"By the handful."

"Has it helped?"

"No."

"That's not good." She paused. "Well, did you have totem poles?"

"Not a chance," Bart said.

"Not even Feather? How come?"

He gave her a pained look. Carrie wasn't sure whether it was the question or his tooth that bothered him more. "I don't know," he said in a barely audible voice.

"Your turn to guess," Carrie said.

"It feels different this winter."

Carrie signaled with her hands for him to say more.

Bart massaged his jaw. "This is no time for this."

Carrie said it should only take a minute.

"It's just different this winter, that's all," Bart said. "It's more...I don't know...more right. It seems to beg for some recognition."

More right? Begs for recognition? Up here you take what you can get.

Bart stood, walked to the bed and lay down and pressed his hands to the side of his jaw.

"Is it throbbing?"

He nodded.

"It should be pulled," Carrie said.

He raised up on one elbow. "Have you ever done that?"

She said no, but that she'd helped her boss with plenty of extractions and added, "Trust me, I know what to do." She couldn't tell if he was satisfied with her answer and tried to soften it by telling him that he didn't have any choice.

He looked at her, his eyes now filled with the distant, surrendering look of pain, and whispered, "You're the doctor."

For the first time, she was teaching him something; she was in charge and enjoyed the role reversal. She leaned toward him and squeezed the toe of his boot. "Just do as I say, and you'll be fine."

She filled a cup with vodka, handed it to him and smiled. "Not a Love Me Tender, but it'll do the trick." Bart smiled weakly back at her. "Okay, down to business," she said. "Down the hatch."

She placed the water pot on the wood stove and poured Bart a second cup of vodka. While he drank, she hung a lantern above the card table and took a pair of pliers from the toolbox beneath the bed and spoon from beside the stove. She watched the water until it boiled and dipped the pliers and spoon in it. Once she was satisfied that they were as sterile as she could hope, she laid them next to the vodka bottle and looked around the small cabin. What else? She placed a roll of toilet paper on the table, seated herself, slipped her right hand into a down mitten and looked into Bart's pained eyes. "Ready?"

Bart swung his feet from the bed and stood, and Carrie wrapped an arm around his waist and pulled him between her legs. She started to hand him the pliers, but stopped. "If I end all this pain will you promise me something?"

Bart looked confused and vulnerable, but Carrie thought she had to do what she had to do. He stared at her, blankly and a bit drunkenly, and said he had no idea what she was talking about.

She didn't blame him, but she didn't care. "Promise?" she said.

"Promise what?"

She pulled him tighter between her legs. "Promise me that if Lola's pregnant you won't kill her pups."

Between the vodka and the pain in his jaw, Bart's words were slurred. "What are you talking about?"

"I think Lola's in a family way."

"You've got to be kidding." He pressed his hands on the sides of his jaw and grimaced. Beads of spittle ran from the corners of his mouth. "There's not another dog within a hundred miles."

"It was the wolf," she said.

"The wolf?" He giggled. "*You've* been drinking."

"I saw them doing it."

He took a clumsy step backward. "For sure?"

Carrie laughed and steadied him tight against her again. "It would have been hard to mistake it for anything else. I didn't tell you because of what you did with the other dogs."

Bart shook his head as though he was having trouble following what she was saying. "Hurry, Carrie. Get on with this. My tooth's killing me."

"Okay, but promise?"

He looked at her with the eyes that never lied. "I promise. Just hurry and get this over with."

She handed him the pliers and told him to clamp them on the tooth that was bothering him. He placed them in his mouth and squeezed them shut.

"You're sure they're on the right one?" she asked.

"Uh huh," he mumbled.

"*Absolutely* sure?"

"Uh huh."

"And you promise you'll let Lola's pups live?"

"Uh huh."

She slipped her gloved hand over the pliers' handles and lifted the spoon and placed its tip at the base of the tooth along his gum.

"It'll only hurt for a second," she said and, without any warning, pressed down with the spoon and pulled on the pliers with all her strength and the tooth came free, followed by a rush of blood and a scream from Bart that filled the cabin and sent Lola scurrying beneath the bed.

Carrie pressed a wad of toilet paper against the dark red hole in the back of Bart's once-perfect smile. "Hold that," she said and filled the cup with vodka and handed it to him. "Bottoms up."

Bart stood trembling between her legs and swallowed the vodka in large gulps.

She took the cup from him and filled it again. "Another."

He drank two more cups as fast as she could fill them and said it was helping the pain although the cabin was beginning to spin.

Carrie stood and eased him to the bed. "In you get," she said and handed him a fresh wad of toilet paper.

He pressed the paper against the wound for a moment and then rolled on his side and pushed his hands between his knees and asked if she could put another log on the stove.

She pulled a blanket and a caribou skin over him and ran her hand over his forehead the way a mother would comfort a feverish child. "Better?"

"Better," he said, and his eyes began to close.

"Promise?" she said.

"She'll be a good mother," Bart mumbled and passed out.

Carrie stood looking down at him. She thought she'd never felt this way about a man before. She leaned over and kissed him on the forehead and whispered, "I think we're getting there."

She stoked the wood stove and pulled on her parka and cap, grabbed her mittens, and clucked at Lola to come out from beneath the bed. "Come on, you naughty girl, let's you and me get a little fresh air. Things are going to be okay. Maybe even better than okay."

11

THE MORNING AFTER Carrie pulled Bart's tooth, snow began to fall, marking the beginning of a storm the likes of which she had yet to see.

The temperature dropped to twenty-seven below zero.

The wind howled and shook the log walls, driving snow in waves against the cabin, the chest-high drifts demanding all Carrie's strength to push open the door and fight her way against the numbing wind to the outhouse.

Bart piled wood in every free space in the cabin and stoked the stove more frequently.

Daylight was nothing more than a few hours of a dull yellow haze glowing from behind the mountains and then the valley was cloaked in darkness once again.

Carrie finally admitted that she felt trapped. "There are times I wonder why I ever..." She stopped.

Bart cocked his head as though he had difficulty hearing her. "Why you ever what?"

There was a worried look in his eyes, and Carrie knew she must choose her answer carefully. "I do love it here, Bart. You know that. Most times I'm glad I'm here, that I've seen this challenge through this far but when it gets like this, well...every once in a while...just occasionally...I wonder why I agreed to stay." She began to sob. "The cold and the dark just get to be too much. They're suffocating. They make it so claustrophobic that I get scared. I worry a lot about what we'd do if one of us had an emergency. I never realized how trapped we'd be." She wiped her tears with her knuckles. "Doesn't it ever scare you? Can't you understand?"

Bart said he understood. "But for me it's simply part of living on the edge." He put a log in the woodstove and then a second. Almost in a whisper, he asked, "If you *could* leave now, would you?"

Carrie sat on the bed and buried her head in her hands. Lola crawled from beneath the table and pressed her nose between her knees. "That's not fair," she said.

"No one said anything about being fair." Bart's voice had taken on an unfamiliar edge. "So, would you leave if you could?"

She stared at the floor and shook her head. "I don't know." For a moment the crackling of the fire mixed with the wind straining the latch on the door were the only sounds in the small cabin. Bart's other women had stayed the whole winter, so why couldn't she? She rubbed her hands over Lola's head and stared into her watery blue eyes. "Push come to shove, the answer's no." She smiled through her tears. "I'm sorry for being such a mess. As long as I've got you and Lola this is my home until the breakup."

"There's nothing to be sorry about," Bart said. "At times it can be very tough, even for me." He sat on the bed and stroked her long blonde curls. "Don't worry, the worst is almost over. The days will be getting longer now." He kissed her on top of her head. "Okay?"

"Okay," she said, and through her tear-filled eyes watched him move to the table and begin planning the totem pole. He drew and re-drew different designs. When he was satisfied, he slid the empty chair close to his and beckoned to her. "Here. Take your mind off the weather and tell me what you think."

She sat with him and studied the piece of paper between his large hands. The images were crude, as though they had been drawn by a child.

"Totems are emblems that remind family members of their ancestry or tell an old family story," he said. "Most of them are found around here or in British Columbia."

Carrie could tell from the look in his eyes that he was excited by his idea and could imagine him standing in front of a group of students, teaching them about totem poles, or how to survive in the bush, or about almost anything for that matter. He was a natural-born teacher who anybody would trust; one that should be able to fit in somewhere.

"They're kind of statements by a family of who they are," he continued. "So our totem should include Lola—"

"And her pups?" Carrie said.

Bart tapped the bottom of the drawing, pointing to four small figures that supported a stylized rendering of a larger animal with sagging, v-shaped, teats. "There they are, and that's Lola." He moved his finger to the next figure. "And there's their father, the ever-powerful wolf." Pointing to the last figure, he said, "And on top, a raven, because they're so wise and are known for warning their people of danger." He ran his finger in a circle around the raven's wings and then its face. "This is the one we see around here with the one good eye."

He slid his hands to his lap. "So, what do you think?"

Carrie hesitated. "It's wonderful but…" She took his hands to steady hers and drew a deep breath. She could feel the now heavy beat of her heart. "What does it say about us?"

"About us?"

"Yes, about us." She tightened her grip on his hands. "I'd like it to say, this is our adventure, our story, our family." She wanted the totem to indicate that Bart loved her, but she'd never said such a thing to a man before and wanted a signal from him that it would be okay.

"Sounds good to me," he said.

We're getting close, she thought, and asked if he would sketch another that included them. As Bart drew, she stood and wrapped an arm around him from behind and pressed her cheek against his. "When do you think Lola will have her pups?"

"Any day now," he said. "It's been at least two months since she and the wolf locked up."

Oh, my God. If it's been over two months and they arrived in October… "Bart, have we missed Christmas?"

"Nope. Today's the twenty-third."

She was startled that he knew the date and asked how he could be so sure.

He pulled a small calendar from the back of the drawer. Each day that had passed since they'd arrived was crossed off with an **X**, but Carrie's thoughts were elsewhere. Not only didn't she know what day it was, she didn't know what was happening in the rest of the world. "Bart, could the United States be at war?"

"If we are, we're better off up here."

"That's not the point, dummy. Could we be at war and you and I not know it?"

Bart said he doubted it. "Whitey would drop us a canister if something's going on we should know about."

"So my mom's okay?"

"Your mom's fine."

"And Hannah, too?"

"And Hannah, too."

"But Whitey didn't tell us about that man who wanted to visit us or about the murder in my apartment building," Carrie said.

"He did in his own way," Bart said. "He sent a message with Feather."

"But he didn't tell us right away."

Bart shrugged. "Because there wasn't a problem."

"You're sure?"

"I'm sure."

While Carrie was relieved by Bart's assurances, other questions were now waiting in line to be asked, questions she thought she should have asked before she set out on this adventure. "How many more of these dreadful winters are you going to do this?"

"I don't know," he said.

"You do have some sort of plan—I mean, for your life—don't you?"

"Do *you*?"

She wondered why it always seemed she ended up doing all the talking. Why he didn't ever answer, didn't open up. But now here she was in the middle of it, talking about what she wanted out of life with a man who was everything she'd ever hoped for, but also a man who might never be tamed to the ways most people would consider normal; a man who couldn't fit in. She sat again and pulled and pushed the table drawer open and closed. "Not a plan maybe, but some day soon I'd like to start a family. I chose to be a dental hygienist over medical school because I didn't want to waste time getting out in the world and settling down and having kids." She paused. "Now it seems as though I've wasted a lot of time making bad decisions."

"We've got a lot in common," Bart said.

Carrie stopped fidgeting with the drawer. "*You've* thought about settling down? About kids?"

He chuckled. "Don't forget, I've already tried that once and having children, or not being able to have them, was the reason I got divorced."

"But if you could have kids, you wouldn't raise them here, would you?"

"A good question, but one I've never had to answer." He stood and began feeding logs into the stove. Carrie thought it was his way of signaling that their discussion had come to an end, but she felt relieved, even satisfied. The seed had been planted.

For a while neither said a word. Bart stared at the flames in the woodstove and poked at the logs. Carrie turned the pages of the small calendar, pretending she was interested in what had passed, when all she cared about was what was to come. She had never felt closer to a man in her entire life and wanted to tell him so many things, even if he only processed them in small increments, one conversation at a time. Something told her that he might be receptive to one more topic. "Have you ever wondered about that guy who attacked you the night we met?"

Bart nodded.

"Why haven't you ever asked about him?"

"You said you didn't want to talk about him."

At times talking with this man was like pulling hens' teeth. "I didn't then, but I do now."

"Okay," Bart said. "You dumped him, and he tried to force himself on you and scared you half to death. Right?"

She looked at him in amazement. "Who told you that?"

"No one. I could tell what happened the night we met."

"But there's something else you should know—about why Jake still haunts me." Once again she began to fidget with the drawer and felt her heart begin to race. "I'd been with him until you and I started to e-mail back and forth; until he began to—"

"You don't have to go into all of this—"

"Please, let me finish. I felt I was partly to blame. I always do. I always feel so guilty, because…" She paused. "I've never met my real father. He and my mom never married. He joined the Navy when he found out Mom was pregnant and she never heard from him again." She moved her hands in circles as though she were stirring something that wouldn't settle for her.

"You okay?" Bart asked.

She nodded and drew a deep breath. "I've never told anyone this except my mom. Not even Hannah. When I was six, my step-father made me…you know…touch him, and when I finally got the courage to tell Mom, he called me a liar and asked my mom how she could believe someone who resented him so. I felt so guilty and confused—"

"And didn't know whether you were making it up because you wanted your real dad or didn't like your step-dad or—"

Carrie was flabbergasted. "How did you know?"

"Because that's the thing bastards like your step-father rely on to keep them safe."

"Wow. You're full of surprises." Tears ran down her cheeks. She drew a finger under her nose. "A few days later Mom and I had another talk and she threw him out."

"Just right," Bart said.

Carrie shook her head. "Well, yes and no. Yes, because I knew what he'd done was bad. No, because I felt I'd ruined Mom's marriage; that it was my fault she got divorced. By the time I was a teenager I'd convinced myself that all men wanted me for was sex. What's worse, I thought that's all I was good for. Can you understand?"

"Yes," Bart said. "I understand. Completely."

She wrapped her arms around his neck and through her sobs muttered, "Thank you."

"Listen. You didn't do anything wrong, Carrie. Nothing at all. Besides, all that stuff's behind you and you're up here where you're safe."

She hoped he was right. "Yes, all that stuff's behind me."

He wiped the tears from her cheeks and kissed her eyes. "Done," he said and asked what was for supper.

Carrie laughed through her tears, a laugh of relief that she'd finally told Bart of her shame. "I guess up here you take what you can get," she said, and with that she and Bart worked hard to keep the camp functioning while they waited for the blizzard to let up.

12

THE STORM RAGED for three days. The wind blew steadily at forty miles an hour, and Bart guessed it gusted to sixty. The cabin walls groaned with each icy blast. Smooth-swept snow drifts reached the roof and covered the lone window in a suffocating sheet of white. Once again Carrie experienced waves of claustrophobia and panic, sensing that this was the storm that would somehow end her life, but she remained tight-lipped, trying to hide her anxiety while she and Bart worked frantically to keep the storm's damage to a minimum.

The howling and shuddering died in the black of Christmas morning as quickly as they had begun, the sudden silence jolting Carrie awake. "What's that?" she said, struggling with the heavy blankets to sit in her bed.

"The storm's quit," Bart said.

"Thank you, God," Carrie said and flopped back onto her pillow. "Thank you, thank you, thank you."

Bart looked at the luminous dial on his watch. "Just in time for breakfast." He slipped from under the covers, lit the lantern above the woodstove, fed logs to the fire and placed the coffee pot on top of the stove.

Carrie pulled the covers over her head. "Breakfast? You've got to be kidding." Her voice was muffled by the layers of blankets and caribou skins. "It's the middle of the night."

"It's almost nine o'clock," Bart said. He lifted the fleece jacket that was stuffed at the base of the door to keep out the draft, pressed his shoulder against the door to force it open and clucked at Lola to come out from her dog house. The husky struggled from her den, pulled her heavy belly a few strides through the deep snow and squatted and made water. Bart glanced at the thermometer: twenty-four below zero. He patted the thigh of his long johns to hurry Lola to the cabin. Once she was inside, Bart crossed his arms over his chest and rubbed his hands up and down his biceps to warm himself as he waited for the coffee to come to a boil. He poured two cups, handed one to Carrie and tapped his against it. "Here's to your first Christmas in Alaska."

"Oh, my God, I forgot," she said and kissed him. "Merry Christmas." She paused. First Christmas in Alaska? Does he really think there'll be others? They had to talk. She took a few warming sips of her coffee, kicked at her clothes that she kept warm by storing them beneath the covers and, very slowly, began to unbutton Bart's long johns.

As Bart rolled toward her, Lola whined and scratched on the door. "Not right now," he coughed.

"I don't think she's feeling well," Carrie said. "She hardly ate at all last night." She took her hand from Bart and looked at the dog. "Bart, there's something wrong with her. Something's sticking out of her."

Bart glanced at Lola, her thick gray tail curled over her back, a shiny grayish-blue sac drooping from her vulva.

"Time to rock and roll. She's having her pups." He threw off the covers and stood and looked about the cabin. He pulled a caribou skin from beside the bed and slid it under the table, then took an armful of logs and arranged them in a square around the skin and knelt and patted the center of the crudely formed whelping box.

Lola scratched the door again. Bart patted the caribou skin a second time, but the husky continued to whine at the door.

"What's wrong?" Carrie said.

"Nothing's wrong. She wants to have her pups in her dog house." He grabbed Lola by the scruff of her neck and pulled her toward the table. "It's too cold for that," he said and forced her into the whelping area. Lola stood still for a moment beneath the table looking up at Bart and Carrie with her pale blue eyes, then curled her head toward her rear end, turned in tight circles, and lay on the caribou skin and uttered a low moan.

Bart moved closer to her and placed a hand lightly on her hip. "The first one's usually the roughest." He reached his other hand toward Carrie. "Flashlight, please." She handed it to him and he shone the light on the water sac. He cradled the small sac in his hands. "It's okay, old girl. Easy does it," he said, and helped the small fetus from the vulva, its black head and body slick and motionless. Lola leaned toward the pup and slapped her tongue from behind its tiny rib cage toward its head in a sweeping motion and suddenly the pup twitched and began to show signs of life. Bart smiled. "Just like spanking a baby."

Carrie put her hands over her face and began to sob. "It's…it's the most beautiful thing I've ever seen. It's incredible." Tears ran freely down her cheeks. She knelt and watched as Lola bit the umbilical cord and cleaned away the placenta. "It's a miracle. She knows exactly what to do." Carrie took the flashlight from Bart and shone it on the pup. "It's a little boy! Bart, she's had a baby boy!" She clapped her hands. "Can I touch her? Do you think she'd mind?"

"I think she'd welcome it."

Carrie rested her hand on the crown of Lola's head and stroked it. "Good girl. You're such a good girl." She sat back on her haunches, smiling as she wiped away her tears. "What do we do now?"

"Have our Christmas breakfast, and watch and wait. It's her show, not ours." As he spoke, Lola took the pup in her mouth, stepped out of the whelping box and again scratched at the door.

"What now?" Carrie asked.

"She wants to make her dog house her den." Again he took Lola by the scruff of her neck and led her back under the table. "Once the pups are a little older—when they're ready for solid food—I think that'll be okay, but not now." He urged the husky back into the whelping box where she lay and nudged the pup near her swollen teats and the pup began to nurse.

Carrie shook her head in wonderment. "I never imagined it would be this beautiful, that she'd be so caring."

"Nature has a lot to teach us; all we've got to do is pay attention," Bart said. "Come on, we've got work to do."

They dressed and began their morning chores, Carrie cooking breakfast, never taking her eyes from the dog for very long; Bart shoveling the door free of the drifted snow, staying close to the sound of Carrie's voice. Within a few minutes Lola turned in circles and another pup began to come. Carrie knelt and watched her clean the new pup and then re-clean the first and exclaimed, "Another boy. Perfect. Just perfect."

THROUGHOUT THE FEW HOURS of muted daylight, Carrie and Bart celebrated each pup as they worked about the cabin and the camp, re-digging the paths to the outhouse, the stream, the sauna and the wood piles, getting things back in order.

Once again submerged in darkness, Bart knelt by the whelping box and placed a shallow bowl of water by Lola's mouth. She lay still, resting for the first time since the morning while her litter fed eagerly, the darkly furred pups tangled at her teats. "What a group," he said. "Enough boys for a basketball team and Thelma and Louise to keep them straight." He looked up with a broad smile. "They're fantastic."

And so are you, Carrie thought, and knelt next to him and wrapped an arm around his waist and kissed him on the cheek. "Thanks for the best Christmas ever. Promise you'll do everything possible to keep them alive?"

"I promise, but they are half-wolf and someday they may want to leave us to live in the wild where they belong, so don't be surprised if it happens."

"Really?" She shook her blonde curls. "I don't want that. I don't like that. I don't like that at all."

"It's not up to us," Bart said. "Besides, you kind of did the same thing when you left La Jolla to come up here."

Carrie thought for a moment and realized that Bart was right. Kind of. She sighed, sat back on her haunches and stared at the pups. "A basketball team and Thelma and

Louise? My, my." She reached to pet her dog. "Well, if they do decide to go, let's hope they're better prepared for their journey than I was."

"Let's hope," Bart said. "But you've made it this far and you're doing fine, although I have to admit there were times when I wondered."

"You did?" Carrie laughed. "I never would have guessed." She laughed again.

A laugh of relief that the storm had ended and the camp was back in order.

A laugh of joy from watching her dog deliver her beautiful pups.

A laugh to celebrate Christmas.

And a laugh of pride for having made it this far in this unforgiving place, with this wonderful man.

She smiled and turned the tables on Bart by cutting the conversation short by saying, "Okay. Now, what's for supper?"

A MONTH PASSED and Carrie stood at the window sipping a cup of tea, watching Bart back slowly from the woods, struggling to drag a large cedar log through the deep snow. He had peeled the bark from the log and it glowed a reddish yellow in the low mid-day sun. Carrie tapped on the window and waved as Bart slowly hauled the log the last few yards through the clearing. He stopped to catch his breath, smiled back at her, staggered a few more yards and dropped the log by the doghouse, the heavy thud drawing one, then two, and eventually all seven pups from their shelter. At first they clawed at the legs of Bart's snow pants and then began to sort out the hierarchy of their pack. Finally, Lola pulled herself from the house, her swollen teats dragging in the snow, and moved against Bart's leg. He held her head against him with a mittened-hand and gently massaged her ears. As Carrie slipped on her snow pants and her parka, Bart pulled the door open and asked if she would bring the drawing of the totem and the pencil.

He paced the length of the log several times, brushing snow from it as he walked. "Twelve feet, plus or minus a few inches," he said, "and close to three feet in diameter. If heft has anything to do with it, it should work just fine." He knelt at the end closest to the cabin, looked at the pups rolling each other over in the snow, and smiled up at Carrie. "You still think you're strong enough to support this motley crew?"

"Not without you," she said.

He took the pencil and began drawing his design on the log, then took a small hatchet from his belt and pulled off a mitten and ran his thumbnail along the hatchet's blade to test its sharpness. "Once I'm done we'll have a potlatch."

"A potlatch?" Carrie said.

"A ceremony, to celebrate things like totems or marriages."

Well, here I go, once and for all, Carrie thought. Ally, ally in free. Here I come, ready or not. She felt adrenaline begin to charge through her. "And what will *we* be celebrating?"

"Finishing the totem," Bart said.

"Anything else?"

Bart shrugged. "Our union?"

"I think we're skipping an important step here," Carrie said.

Bart began chopping at the drawings of Carrie and him at the base of the log.

Carrie waited for him to say something more. When he didn't, she asked if he'd heard her, but he still didn't look up or answer. She raised her voice as though she had to speak louder over the silence of the wilderness. "Bart, I said I think we're skipping an important step."

He studied the drawing and made a short chop with the hatchet. Carrie reached down and took it from him. Holding the small but lethal weapon gave her a feeling of power, something she needed at this moment; needed badly. She turned the blond wood handle in her mittens and studied the shiny edge of the blade. Her heart was beating heavily; her breath filled her lungs with warmth. "Bart?" she said.

Bart whisked snow from the log and looked up.

"Bart," she said again and sighed. "Oh, boy." She paused a moment. "Do you love me?"

Bart's eyes softened as Lola leaned against him and licked his cheek. He wrapped his arm around the dog's thickly furred neck and held her close against him. "It should be pretty obvious."

"Are you *in love* with me?"

Bart stroked the husky's shoulder. "If wanting you to be my companion for the rest of my life is what you call being in love, then the answer is yes. Definitely yes."

Carrie's eyes filled with tears. "And might I ask why you haven't said something before?"

Bart stood and swept snow from the knees of his pants. "You never asked."

"Oh." Once again Bart's law.

"And what about you?" he said.

Carrie had never told a man what she was about to tell Bart, and she hesitated and stalled to build her courage. "What about me?"

"Come on, Carrie." He took the hatchet from her and set it on top of the log. "How about you?"

Carrie turned in a circle and blew a stream of air through her mouth. It formed a little cloud between Bart and her that quickly disappeared. "I think I've been in love with you since the moment I first saw you, but I'd done so many dumb things with other men that it took me a long time to know that we were okay, that I'd finally found the man I'd been searching for."

Bart put his mittened hands on her shoulders. "And that feeling will last forever?"

"Forever," Carrie said. "And you?"

"For as long as I live," he said, and squeezed her shoulders tight. "You feel that way even out here?"

"Yes, even out here," and her mouth was hard against Bart's, releasing all her fears, pouring out her sense of relief, pushing against his searching kiss to let him know how truthful her answer was, how desperately she loved and wanted him, and how thankful she was that he and his beloved wilderness had saved her from her meaningless life in southern California and from so many other things. So many, many other things.

13

THE WOLF DIDN'T MOVE. His legs were punched in deep drifts at the edge of the sea of white in front of him, his sleek body nothing more than a shadow against the darkness of the tree line. A frigid breeze lifted a dusting of snow from the thick hair of his shoulders and along his back. His almond-shaped eyes shone crystal yellow in the light of the quarter moon.

He lowered his head and stretched his neck forward as a Sitka doe and her fawn appeared in the clearing not fifty yards from him. He watched the doe pause, lift her head and raise her ears to sense for danger while her fawn waved her large tail freely and pranced a short distance from her. The doe tiptoed in the wolf's direction. Her fawn followed, her head close by her mother's hindquarters. Fifteen yards from the wolf, the doe stopped again, craned her neck and looked directly at him, while the younger deer stepped slowly toward him, more curious than wary.

Daredevil remained motionless.

The doe switched her tail, a signal that she was readying to bolt and with two explosive strides that sent clouds of snow flying behind him Daredevil was on top of her fawn, his powerful jaws locked on the small deer's frail, brownish-gray neck. Her spindly legs flailed, her small hooves failing to get purchase, and instantly she was buried on her side, the wolf covering her with his body, waiting for her life to empty into a sweet-smelling well of blood boring deep into the snow.

Daredevil raised his eyes and watched the doe sprint away. When she was a safe distance from him, she stopped and pawed with one of her fore-hooves, trying to attract the wolf to her, to divert him, to save her offspring's life. The wolf tightened his grip on the fawn's jugular and waited for her struggling to stop while the doe coughed at him and continued to stomp her hoof in the snow. Come, take *me*, she seemed to be saying. When the fawn was finally still, Daredevil stood and growled and the doe bounded toward the woods, head thrown back, back arched, tail held high, its under-hairs showing bright white in the moonlight like a flag of surrender.

The wolf lowered his head as the shadow of a raven circling across the moon passed fleetingly over the snow. The bird settled in a lone tree at the edge of the woods and cocked his head, then puffed his shaggy ebony throat feathers and began to preen. Daredevil looked up for a moment and stared at the bird and then ripped at the fawn's belly and began to eat.

WITHIN THE HOUR Daredevil picked his way through the woods and stopped at the edge of the clearing at Bart and Carrie's cabin. A gray-black cloud drifted across the moon throwing all into darkness except the flickering reflection of the woodstove showing through the cabin window. The wolf paused, pricked his ears and worked his nose, and crept silently forward.

He stopped at the mouth of the doghouse and cocked his head as a low growl came from within. Lola's scent and the smell of her pups drew him a step forward. The growling continued. Daredevil lay on his stomach, ears flattened against his head, and inched toward the small opening where he could feel the warmth of Lola's body and see her pups nestled against her. He drew his lips back and showed his teeth. Lola stopped growling and thumped her tail. Her pups thrashed and crawled toward the wolf.

He opened his large jaws, tucked his stomach once and then a second and a third time and regurgitated the freshly eaten meat from the fawn. At first the pups licked at the warm pile, its steaming, sweet odor filling their space, and then began to eat, crawling and sliding on the vomit to find their share.

Daredevil heard a sharp sound come from the cabin—the sound of the woodstove being stoked—and pulled back from the opening and bolted through the deep snow to the cover of the woods. In the distance he heard the caw of the raven and slowly switched his tail, then turned and loped through the trees, the moonlight casting narrow bands of shadows across his path. Atop his familiar hillside, less than a mile from his pack, Daredevil sat, raised his eyes toward the moon, called one long, soulful howl for his mate and turned and disappeared into the blackness of his den.

As the howl reached the McFee campsite, Lola lowered her muzzle between her paws with a grunt of contentment as her litter burrowed against her once again, their small bellies stretched tight with their first taste of solid food.

Inside the cabin, Carrie rolled toward Bart beneath the heavy layer of blankets. "I wonder what he's trying to tell her."

Bart wrapped his arms around Carrie's waist and moved closer to her. "I guess he's saying he wants her with him. Like me with you. It's only natural."

14

TIME DRAGGED. The darkness imprisoned Bart and Carrie for all but a few hours each day. Its suffocating presence disrupted their sense of time, their equilibrium with day and night. They checked their watches frequently. Bart used the light that shone through the cabin window to split wood and carve the totem while Carrie filled her days cooking or tidying and re-tidying the cabin or reading and memorizing poetry. Tending to Lola and her pups and dreams of a brighter, warmer future cheered her, but the sameness of her routine and the oppressive blackness caused her mind to wander. In her bluest moments she worried that her life in the wilderness was beginning to be no different from the one she'd abandoned in southern California—repetitive and aimless—and fretted that maybe she could never be satisfied, that she would always be a restless soul. Each time she had these thoughts, she heard Hannah's voice, "You think you're bored here? Wait until you've been up there for three or four months. You'll be going stark raving mad!"

One morning, well into the short but dismal month of February, she poured herself a cup of coffee, handed Bart a bowl of oatmeal and asked if they were a couple of misfits.

"What makes you ask that?" Bart said.

"Because I was never really satisfied or happy in La Jolla. I always felt I was on the fringe of what was really going on. Not like an outcast, exactly, but not in any inner circle, either."

"I wouldn't worry about it," Bart said. "If you're a misfit one place, you're a misfit everywhere, and I don't think that's the case with you. You just didn't have any purpose in your life."

"And what about you?"

"I'll admit there was a time when nothing was right for me either, but this life convinced me that I can fit in almost anywhere, if there's something at stake."

"So, why haven't you tried something more conventional? You're going to have to do it someday, you know."

"Don't worry, I'll be ready, but right now I like it better up here." He finished his breakfast and took the rifle from behind the stove, loaded it and slipped a handful of cartridges in his pants pocket. "I'm going to look for a deer. We're getting low on food for Lola and we could use a little change in diet, too." He checked his watch and said he should be at the south meadow before it gets light, and should be back before dark. He took his heavy parka from the peg on the door and asked if she wanted to come along.

"You know I don't like killing things," Carrie answered. "I may snowshoe for awhile if the weather holds, but we need to talk more about this when you get back. It's about our future after all."

CARRIE CLEANED the breakfast bowls, straightened the bed, swept the cabin floor and poured another cup of coffee. She sat at the table and reread the Whitman poetry that

Bart and she had read the night before and tried to convince herself that the breakup wasn't that far away, that everything was going to turn out fine, that in a few months they would be on their way home, back to a new life for both of them, finding a way to fit in. She smiled. And together they'd find meaning and purpose in their new lives.

She stood and stared out the window. A thin red line of light rose from behind the mountains. She bundled herself in her heaviest cold weather gear. Once outside she checked the thermometer. Thirty below. She laughed as she thought of Whitey's parting words: "Enjoy the Riviera." Some Riviera!

She knelt by the doghouse and reached around the partition that shielded Lola and her pups from the wind. Her mitten first settled on the ball of pups and then on Lola's side. Carrie patted her, heard her tail thump on the straw-covered floor and was convinced all was well. She fastened her snowshoes and scanned the horizon for signs of foul weather. In the distance low clouds dumped snow at the base of Mount Logan, but Carrie thought the weather near camp would hold, at least for a few hours until it was dark again, and she set out through the thick woods toward the direction of the wolf's nightly howling. As she snowshoed, clumps of snow occasionally fell like large white pillows, exploding in a misty haze at her feet. Once she reached the meadow where she'd seen the wolf locked with Lola the wind began to twist the snow in small spirals. Carrie wiped her dark glasses with increasing frequency. Oblivious to the worsening weather she traipsed back and forth for the better part of an hour, covering every inch of the open space, hoping to be able to tell Bart that she'd found the tracks of the wolf; maybe even that she'd caught a glimpse of him. By the time she'd decided that her hunt was fruitless the sun had begun to slip behind the mountains and darkness had begun to fill the woods. She hurried back to camp, the snow swirling in small clouds with the building wind; the wind driving the cold through the protection of her wool mask, drilling a dull pain into her sinuses. Traveling was slow and uncomfortable, but she assured herself that she would soon see the light from the cabin to guide her and comfort her and pressed on through the darkness and the frigid gale when she thought she heard a shot, muffled and disguised in the wind's howling, but a shot nonetheless.

She stopped and cocked her head as though if she stood still and listened carefully enough the sound would be repeated. She waited but heard nothing but the wind as it coursed through the trees and she snowshoed as fast as she could in the direction of the cabin. Frozen branches, some heavy with snow, others brittle and bare, brushed and scraped her facemask. When she finally came to the campsite, the cabin was nothing more than a black mass huddled in the darkness. Cold, remote, unfamiliar.

And there was no sign of Bart.

Carrie worked her way out of her snowshoes and hurried inside. She lit the lanterns and set the fire and the cabin began to warm and welcome her, although, oddly, it seemed too big for her alone. She stood, still dressed in her puffy, quilted clothes, warming her hands as she watched the fire build and wondered what was keeping Bart. She thought he must have shot a deer; that it would take a while to clean it and drag it home in the foul weather. "But he never leaves the cabin unattended for this long," she said aloud. But it had been dark for less than an hour and there was no cause for alarm. After all, he'd survived many of these winters before without any problems. Again she spoke aloud to comfort herself and said, "Time to get down to business."

She took the flashlight and Lola's bowl and pushed through the drifted snow to the locker behind the outhouse. She swept a cushion of snow from its heavy lid, lifted it and played the light across its contents: one full bag and one open bag of kibble on the left; a neatly butchered pile of meat on the right. She studied the cache for a moment. There wasn't enough to feed Lola until the breakup, and she wondered what the puppies would eat when they'd been weaned and hoped Bart had been successful in his hunt.

She scooped kibble into the bowl and reached for a piece of meat but decided against it. Not tonight, she thought. Save some, just in case. As she hurried back to the cabin she yelled over the howling wind at Lola that it was supper time. The husky and her pups crawled from their shelter and met her at the cabin door, the puppies wagging their small tails. Carrie led all inside and set the bowl of kibble on the floor. She stripped off her outer clothing and sat on the bed to watch the pups chase and roll each other about the cabin. The blackest of the litter, the one she'd named Louise, tugged on the lace of her boot, then lay alongside her foot and looked up at her with gray-black eyes. Carrie held her against her boot to measure her and muttered, "My, how you've grown." She lifted the pup to eye level, kissed her on the nose and stepped carefully over the others holding Louise tight against her. For the first time since she'd arrived she studied the larder and took inventory. Their food was low, too. Again she hoped Bart had been successful. She rubbed her cheek against the puppy's fur and walked to the window, hoping to see Bart's dark form against the snow.

What is keeping him?

She pushed the door open and scooted Lola and her pups outside, slipped on her parka and joined them, moving the light of the flashlight from puppy to puppy. As they began to file into their doghouse she searched the darkness for a sign of Bart, but the yellow beam of her light failed to penetrate the swirling snow. "Bart? Bart! Where are you?" she called as loudly as she could. "It's time for supper."

Suddenly she heard a sound. "Bart?"

No answer and then she heard the sound a second time. It came from above. She looked up and shone her light on the raven as he landed on a bare limb of a cottonwood. The bird tilted his head and opened his thick beak and cawed loudly and then settled deep within himself, his one good eye blinking in the flashlight's beam.

The bird's presence caused Carrie to shudder. "What is it?" she screamed. "Can't you see he's not home?"

The raven shook his head and pulled it further between his shoulders.

She switched off the light and yelled, "You're no help. Go bring him home. Please, go and guide him back to me."

15

THE FIRST TIME Carrie checked her watch it was four o'clock, the time she always fed Lola. From then on she glanced at her watch every five minutes and looked out the window, straining to see through the wind-driven snow swirling in the darkness. More than once she pushed open the door against the storm's force and called Bart's name.

At six she opened a can of beef stew and stirred it fitfully in the heavy iron pot. It was time for Bart to come home, have his supper and talk of his hunt; perhaps read some poetry and join her in their bed.

Another empty hour passed but Carrie kept her hopes up, reassuring herself that Bart was okay, that he knew every inch of these woods and how to survive anything and everything. After all, he'd made it this far, over all these years, without a problem and he had the rifle and the grizzlies were hibernating, so nothing could possibly go wrong. She ladled a serving of stew into her bowl and placed it on the table and scooped a glass of water from the water bucket and sat. For the first time since she'd been in the wilderness she said grace to bless her good fortune, ending with, "And please, God, send him home tonight. I love him, and I need him. We're just beginning. Amen."

She sat for a moment with her head bowed and her hands folded in her lap and let out a loud sigh and then screamed for help. She opened the door and called to Bart once more, then clucked at Lola and her pups to join her in the cabin. "Just for a moment; for a little company."

Once all were inside, she chided them to behave, calling each by name. Thelma. Louise. Bear. Wolf. Raven. Salmon. And finally, Sinatra, the one with pale blue eyes like his mother. She picked at her food, emptied her water and poured herself a cup of vodka. As her food satisfied her hunger and the vodka took its hold, she thought she was experiencing a moment of clarity like few she'd ever had: Bart would not be coming home.

But the clarity quickly turned to confusion, to hope and then to desperation. She thought back to what had sounded like a rifle shot, although she couldn't swear it was. She had assumed that if it were a shot, it was Bart dispatching a deer but now she wasn't so sure. Maybe it was someone else. For an instant she panicked. Bill Davies or Davis or whatever his name was, or Jake? Nonsense, she thought. Don't be foolish. No one in their right mind would be out here in weather like this; no one except for Feather, but she would have stopped by the cabin to say hello. Wouldn't she?

She poured herself another inch of vodka and opened the door and called again for Bart, but her voice had lost its conviction. She checked the thermometer before shutting the door. Good Lord! No one, not even her gorgeous, gentle adventurer could survive for long at thirty below. She sat and drained her drink, for a moment pressed the cup to her forehead and then threw it against the door. "God damn it!" she screamed. "This can't be happening. It's not fair. I can't live without you, Bart, so come home, God damn it, Bart, and come home now!"

She watched the aluminum cup roll across the floor; watched the pups begin to chase it and box at it with their paws. For a moment she didn't care what they did, didn't care if what she was feeling was selfish, if it didn't take into account that Bart might be in trouble and needed her help. She was alone and terrified. She was afraid she couldn't live until the breakup without him, the breakup that now seemed years away.

She returned Lola and her litter to their shelter, shone the light about the campsite and gave one last call for Bart. Wait until daylight, she told herself. There's nothing else to do.

CARRIE WOKE from her shallow sleep to each crackling of the woodstove, to each howl and shudder of the wind. From time to time she called Bart's name and reached for him to feel his warmth, moving her hand in searching circles beneath the covers, then pulling it away from the cold space where he should be sleeping, uttering a sharp draw of breath and a cry of "Oh, no."

Early morning she rose and fumbled in the dark to stoke the woodstove. She crawled back in bed and pressed her fists hard against her cheeks and cried; cried for Bart and cried because she was afraid, not only of what life would be like without him, but because she'd never been alone before.

Quite the contrary, she thought. She'd always had her mom around her, and cousins or friends, to make up for no brothers or sisters. Especially no sisters. She'd had all those girls who swam with her in high school and at USC as friends and companions. And, of course there was always

Hannah, her best friend. She wiped her eyes and her upper lip. Hannah, who stuck by her while she searched for the man of her dreams, getting it wrong until she found Bart...or he found her...or they found each other. With this thought, she began to heave with sobs again.

After another unsettled hour of grieving and wrestling with her dilemma, Carrie gave in to the need to pee and lit the lantern above the stove, pulled on her warm clothes and trudged through the darkness and the waist-high snow to the outhouse. Outside the privy she folded her cap above her ears and listened for signs of life. Any sign at all. The silence was heightened by the darkness. She looked in the cottonwood for the raven but he, too, was gone. She cupped her mittens by her mouth and screamed, "Can anybody hear me? Can anybody help me?"

All was silent.

She waded back to the cabin, filled the coffee pot and set it on the woodstove and then bellowed at the top of her lungs, "Good God almighty, won't someone help me? I'm scared shitless and alone. All alone." Again she began to cry, her sobs pulling hard at her already aching stomach muscles.

She poured herself coffee, sat on the bed and held the warm cup between her hands and gazed absent-mindedly through her tears at the comforting flames of the wood-stove. Bart would tell her to shape up. So would Hannah. She couldn't let them down. She nodded to herself and said aloud, "I *can* make it. I *must*. Just keep it simple, focus on the essentials, and I'll do it. Loneliness never killed anyone." She sipped her coffee. "Or did it?"

She pulled on her outer gear and left the cabin. The sky glowed red and her optimism resurfaced. It would be light in an hour and then she'd find Bart and somehow he'd be okay. She clapped her mittens together to strengthen her resolve. She shoveled the paths, first to the outhouse and then the sauna, and cleared a narrow passage to the stream and chopped it open with the axe, lingering for a moment, staring at the swirling black water and listening to its quiet song. It was the only sign or sound of life of any kind and once again she knew her worst fears would come true but she had to look because maybe, just maybe...

Within the hour, muted daylight began to fill in the details of the valley and Carrie snowshoed through the woods, stopping frequently to search for a sign of her gorgeous adventurer. At the meadow where she thought Bart would have hunted, the snow from the night before lay like a freshly drawn sheet over a welcoming place of rest. The wind had flattened all of the open space except for a smoothed mound in the far corner of the field.

Carrie was afraid to look but knew she must.

She drew a deep breath to collect more courage than she had ever called upon before, but couldn't take a step. She stared at the mound of snow, silent and peaceful in the gray winter light. She shivered at what she was imagining. This couldn't be...

Her thoughts were interrupted by the cawing of the raven circling in a thermal high above her. "I know. I know," she called to him. "Just give me a minute to gather my thoughts." Her destination was no more than one hundred yards from her and she marked her progress to take her mind off what she was doing; to give her strength.

Ten yards.

Twenty.

Thirty.

When she had covered eighty yards a buff and black form sprang from behind the tomb-like mound and squared itself on all fours. The look in the wolf's slanted yellow eyes held Carrie in mid-stride, but before she could react the wolf wheeled and sprinted to the woods and disappeared in the maze of leafless trees and blow-down. Carrie slapped her mittened hands against her face mask. What was he doing, she wondered, and muttered, "Oh, no. Oh, God, no!" and trotted clumsily to the bulging snow.

Where the wolf had been lying the tamped snow was maroon with blood. Carrie dropped to one knee and placed her hands together in prayer. "Bart?" she whispered. Her heart pounded heavily and she angrily swept snow from the wolf's prey convinced she would discover the inevitable answer to her mystery but uncovered nothing more than a half-eaten deer.

CARRIE RETURNED to the cabin as darkness began to shroud the valley. She stood for a moment and watched the soft gray glowing slowly disappear behind the mountains. She checked her watch. Two-fifteen. She unclasped her snowshoes and hung them on the pegs by the door and ran a mittened hand over the space where Bart always hung his. What now? She called to Lola and her litter and while she waited for them to emerge from their shelter and go about their business she collected an armful of wood.

Once she'd attended to the woodstove and the pups had settled on the caribou skins that covered the rough wood floor she made herself a cup of tea and pulled the calendar from the table drawer. February twenty-third. Hannah would turn thirty in a few days. Carrie wondered if she'd ever see her friend again and then wondered if Bart had run away from her because he couldn't live with the commitment he'd made to her. She shook her head. Something had happened to him, although she had no idea what that could have been.

She tapped the small calendar against her open hand. She thought she was certain of two things: looking for Bart with all the snow and the vast area around their camp was hopeless; and, without the rifle, there was no way to hunt or defend herself. She addressed Lola and her litter as if they were aware of her predicament. "But don't worry, I haven't come this far to fail. Nor to die."

AFTER SHE'D FINISHED cleaning up her supper, Carrie took stock of her situation. For a change, her issues weren't the men in her life, or her hairstyle, or the lecherous dentist she worked for. There was only one issue: whether or not she had enough food to last her until the breakup.

She sharpened a stubby yellow pencil with the kitchen knife, poured a second cup of tea and sat with the calendar. She crossed out February 23rd and drew a circle around May 15th and counted the days in between. Eighty days, more or less, she thought, and then allowed ten days for hiking out. She needed food for ninety days. Food for about three months.

She stood and counted her canned goods: two cases of beef stew; three cases of Chunky Soup; three loose cans of turkey stew. Sixty-three cans in all, plus a half-can of powdered eggs. She sat and slid a piece of paper from the desk drawer and calculated that if she ate three meals a day she would need about 270 meals to survive. "Jesus," she gulped, "I've only got half of that." She re-calculated her needs eating only two meals a day and did the math a second time to make sure she had figured correctly. She was still almost a month short.

She clenched her curls and pulled them tight and cried, "I'm going to starve to death and so are the dogs. What am I to do?" She stood and turned in a circle. "Eat like a bird, drink lots of water and pray. There's nothing else."

But what about Lola? She could feed her half her normal ration, but that would only work for a while and left nothing for her pups. Bart had been right about killing the sled dogs and she wondered if she had the rifle would she now do the same? God, how things have changed.

She committed to her plan and, although she had no idea of what to do for the dogs, she thought with luck at least she might survive and make it back to civilization and wondered what that would be like. Would her life fall back into the same boring routine? How would she prevent that? What would she do differently without Bart? She had no idea, and when she wasn't thinking about him and how much she loved and missed him and how unfair it was that he'd disappeared, she thought about nothing else but what was in store for her if she could survive until the breakup.

THE FOLLOWING MORNING Carrie fought her way through the dark to the outhouse, the drifted snow shimmering and rolling like the swells of an ocean. Once back at the cabin, she dug an opening in the snow that covered the doghouse. "Good morning, everybody. Time to rise and shine," she said, and knelt and peered in and then screamed, "Holy Jesus, where are you?"

She grabbed the flashlight from the cabin and shone it first in the doghouse and then back and forth across the snow and called for Lola. "Oh my God, they're gone! Not Lola, too. No! She was…was part of our family and so were her pups." Had they left her for the wild? And, if so how? She never dreamed this would happen, even though Bart had warned her more than once that it might; that it was only natural. She stomped her boots and began to cry. "Jesus, but this is a godforsaken place. One minute I'm worrying about how I'm going to feed them and the next minute I'm all alone. Trapped and alone."

She swept the light across the snow and called for the dogs once more when she heard the flapping of the raven's wings. She looked up and trained her light on him as he settled in the cottonwood, his bright ebony eye glittering in the flashlight's beam. "What now? What do you want from me?"

The raven stretched its neck and gave a long, hoarse caw and pulled his head between his shoulders.

"You're no help, you stupid bird. I'll work it out myself." She turned to enter the cabin but stopped and sighed. "Sorry. I'm not myself right now. You're the only friend I've got."

The raven tipped his head once as though he agreed.

She remembered how strange she thought Bart's comment was when they first arrived and he'd told her that the raven was a friend. And now he was her friend, too. Again she thought how things had changed and shone the light on him and flicked it off. "The good news is, now the dogs won't starve." She pulled open the cabin door and muttered, "The bad news is, I just might."

Inside the cabin she stoked the fire and collapsed on the bed and debated how long it would take her to snowshoe to the Wrangell Mountain Camp. She began to fill a rucksack with cans of stew, a poncho, matches, Bart's small hatchet and extra clothing then threw the rucksack on the bed. "Who am I kidding?" she said aloud. "It could take three weeks or more. I'd never make it. I'd freeze to death for sure. Or starve. Or both."

She sat on the bed and sobbed and asked herself what an animal would do. She drew a deep breath to help gather her thoughts. The answer was simple: he'd stay where he had water, food and shelter, and travel when it was safe. She nodded. "That's it. That's what will keep me alive."

She put a log in the stove and unpacked the rucksack. Her words came almost as a chant. "Keep busy. Take care of yourself. Stick to the routine." She was as determined as she was scared and heartbroken. She knew she mustn't quit, that she was able enough to see it through. All it would take was applying what she'd learned from Bart. And discipline. And some luck.

WHEN SHE FINISHED her first day of chores she decided that taking the very best care of herself included enjoying life's little pleasures. That was the least she could do. Inside the sauna she lit the lantern and the woodstove and watched as the ice she had placed in the galvanized tub began to melt and steam. While she waited for the water and the cabin to warm, she studied herself with the hand mirror that hung on the wall. Her face below her ski goggles' protection was dark brown from wind and sun. Another line of brown ran along her forehead where her goggles were separated from her cap. Her eyes were tear-puffed and her matted curls hung over her shoulders like knotted strands of wool. She didn't look at all as she had when she'd arrived five months before, yet the difference wasn't only cosmetic. There was something else. She wondered if it was the yellow light of the lantern, and knew it wasn't, but didn't know exactly what it was.

The sauna warmed and she spent a long time bathing. When she was through, she jogged to the cabin and poured a small drink of vodka. "Okeydokey," she said. "Clean clothes and then what's for supper? Chunky Soup or Chunky Soup?" She threw her hands in the air in surrender. She had to stop talking to herself. She thought she sounded like she was stark raving mad.

When she was through eating she tried to read some of Walt Whitman's poetry but the words would not settle on the page and she undressed and crawled under the thick layer of blankets, the cabin lit only by the flickering flames of the woodstove. She calmed herself and listened to the distant call of the wolf and wondered if Lola was howling with him. She slipped from the bed and into her boots and parka and opened the door to hear the howling more clearly.

The wind raised snow in small twisters about the cabin. The clouds had disappeared and in the moon-lit night she could make out the silhouette of the raven perched in the cottonwood by the outhouse. "Taking care of me?" she called. The raven raised his wings slightly and tucked his head. "Well, thanks. At least someone cares."

Carrie looked above her. The sky was ablaze with the Northern Lights, their maroon and lime-green washes hanging silently over the silhouette of Mt. Logan. Through her tears she could make out the stars and constellations that Bart had said were her new friends: the North Star, the Little Bear, Andromeda, the Charioteer, the Lesser Dog. As he'd once suggested, they looked close enough to touch and she raised a hand to the heavens, hoping she might draw strength from all that he had taught her, from all that was around her, from all she had fallen in love with.

16

FEBRUARY CAME TO A CLOSE. Not a day passed without Carrie mourning the loss of Bart and Lola and her pups. The emptiness of her life was overwhelming. In the mornings she would recite poetry, using the discipline of memorizing her favorite poems to keep her mind engaged. While she thought it strange, she continued to talk aloud to comfort herself with the sound of her own voice. After her breakfast she swept and neatened the cabin and checked the lanterns—frequently topping them off with kerosene, all to keep everything tidy and in order—and shoveled the paths to the outhouse, the sauna and the stream. At least twice each day she chopped the frozen stream open for water and restocked the firewood by the stove. And, when the weather permitted, at midday she snowshoed for several hours to escape the confines of the cabin while most evenings she bathed to break the boredom.

On the occasions she was visited by the raven she pretended to engage him in conversation, telling him how lonely she was, how much she'd loved Bart and still did, how she wished the breakup would hurry up and come and how damn hungry she was all day long.

At the end of her first week alone she brushed the snow from the lid of the locker behind the outhouse and peered inside. She begrudgingly accepted the fact that without its contents she might starve and counted the small cuts of dog meat tucked in the far corner. Twelve meals, she thought, but only if there was no other way for she couldn't stand the idea of eating the sled dogs. She reached in the opened bag of kibble and took a few pellets and ate them. It was a little sandy, a bit fishy tasting, but not that bad. She rolled the top of the bag closed and carried it back to the cabin.

THE FIRST MORNING that the sun began to climb from behind the mountains while Carrie was making breakfast—a small portion of beef stew mixed with kibble—she felt a new sense of hope and optimism. "Brighter days are ahead," she said, and added, "I hope."

She reached for the calendar that she had nailed behind the stove and marked the day as she had every day since Bart had disappeared. "Two more months. Two more long, lonely God damn months." She sighed and picked at her food and sipped her coffee. "It's like a prison sentence." It was so much work just to stay alive and she finally understood why Bart had said companionship was a key to survival; understood why Feather and the others.

She rested her chin in her hands and stared out the cabin's lone window and began to cry, wondering if she had an endless supply of tears. She banged her cup on the table and stood. "Enough of that. No more feeling sorry for yourself. There's work to be done."

She finished tidying the cabin and stepped through the snow to the outhouse. The new morning light buoyed her mood, relieving the tension of the damned darkness. She looked up to the cottonwood tree, smiled and waved at the raven. "Beautiful day, huh?" The bird didn't move or blink. Carrie took this to be a form of agreement and laughed and looked about her, again enjoying the luxury of light. She finished in the outhouse and searched the several woodpiles for logs that Bart had split for the stove, but there were none. Good Lord, she thought, another thing to do, then scolded herself to look on it as something new, something to break the routine.

She carried an armful of logs to a spot near the cabin door and set one on its edge in the snow. She studied the log for a moment and straightened it a bit with the head of the axe. Her first half-hearted chop hit well off-center, barely penetrating the wood. This was a lot harder than Bart had made it look. She squared her feet, tapped the center of the log with the axe and raised it above her head and swung it with all her might. The axe glanced off the log and sliced through the pant leg of her snow pants, its blade burying deep in her left calf.

She screamed with pain and horror as blood spurted from the gash in her pants, and clamped her mitten over the wound and hobbled to the cabin. Small maroon pools of blood and pink clumps of snow followed her to the bed where she sat and willed herself to remain calm; knowing that what she did next was a matter of life or death.

Mittens and hat off.

Parka unzipped and removed.

She leaned forward, her face flushed by the warmth of the woodstove. Left boot unlaced and gently—ever so gently—pulled off.

Blood ran freely down her leg and into her heavy gray wool sock.

Right boot off in a hurry.

Ski pants suspenders un-snapped and left leg pulled free.

For the first time she saw the size of the wound and the constant flow of blood through her long johns, and knew she was in serious trouble, that she had to stem the flow of blood.

But how?

She finished taking off her ski pants and lifted her butt from the bed and worked her long johns down her legs and pulled them from her feet and knotted the clean leg at the top of her calf and twisted it until the blood flow slowed to a trickle.

Now clean the wound.

She reached for the small bucket next to the stove and dragged it between her feet and splashed water over her calf and wiped the blood away with her open hand and watched the pinkish water trickle down her leg and mix with the dark blood that covered her ankle and foot.

She studied the wound. The gash was no longer than her hand, but she could see the white of her shin bone.

"Now what?"

She held tight to the tourniquet, thought for a moment, and stood. She felt lightheaded and waited until she regained her bearings before feeding two logs into the stove.

She poured some water into a metal cup and set it on the stove and took the small sewing kit and scissors that Bart kept in the table drawer and set them on the bed, then laid a table knife by them and sat. When the water began to bubble she chose the largest needle and dipped it in the cup.

She let go of the tourniquet to thread the needle and blood began to run freely once more.

She worked quickly to find the eye of the needle, knotted off a length of thread and twisted the tourniquet tight.

Again she washed the wound, this time pouring water directly over it.

She rested her left foot on her right thigh, slipped on a mitten and leaned toward the stove. She opened the front gate, and held the blade of the table knife in the flames until it turned red hot and then pressed the knife blade directly in the wound.

And screamed for holy Jesus.

She fought to hold the knife in place and screamed again, the smell of burning flesh rising about her and then she vomited her small breakfast and dropped the knife on the floor.

The cabin began to move about her. She closed her eyes and willed the world to come to rest.

Slowly she loosened the tourniquet and stared at the blackened wound. The bleeding appeared to have stopped. She dipped a cup in the water bucket and took several large gulps and then swallowed four or five aspirin tablets—she couldn't be sure how many; she was having trouble focusing—and limped to the shelf that held the vodka bottle.

"No," she said and tossed the bottle on the bed and fished a tee-shirt from Bart's box of clothes and sat. "I need a clear head for one more thing."

She washed and wiped the wound clean with the tee-shirt and reached for the needle and thread. She heard her mother's favorite admonition, a stitch in time saves nine, and then muttered to herself, "Okeydokey, Carrie, suck it up and save nine," and began to stitch the wound closed.

The straight needle made the task difficult and she envied the proper suture instruments that were so familiar to her in her former life. She thought she should tie off every stitch, then thought she'd never get through it all, and forced the needle through her skin again and squeezed the skin together and sewed it shut and drew a deep breath and repeated the process, sixteen times in all, each time the pain growing sharper and more intense, until finally she knotted off the thread.

She was finished, by God. Finished.

She studied her work briefly and bandaged her leg with Bart's tee-shirt. She was drowsy from pain and the loss of blood and wanted to lie down, to sleep, just for a while, until the pain subsided. She looked down at the floor, her boots and bloody ski pants and long johns and one heavy, blood-soaked wool sock lying in a pile at her feet, her small deposit of vomit on the floor by them. She thought she'd clean up everything when she woke and slid beneath the covers, took one long pull on the vodka bottle and screwed the cap back on. Her eyes began to close, the crackling woodstove and the bright kerosene lantern suddenly going out of focus, and she fell asleep.

CARRIE WOKE HOURS LATER, tucked in a ball beneath her covers, shivering, her wound throbbing.

She hobbled to the stove and stoked the fire and lifted the bucket to her mouth and drank in large gulps, water spilling down her chin and onto her turtleneck. She took more aspirin and crawled over the end of the bed and back under the covers. As the cabin began to warm she adjusted her pillows and soon was fast asleep once again.

A few hours later she went through these same steps once more.

The next time she woke, something was different. Shit, she thought, the lamp over the stove was out of kerosene. Limping the few paces to stoke the fire exhausted her and she dropped to her knees. The woodpile was almost all gone. She set three logs in the stove, fumbled for the aspirin bottle and took another handful and got back under her covers, promising herself that she'd get more firewood and fill the lamp in a little while, when she felt a little stronger.

The darkness of night returned and the fire dwindled to nothing but a few red embers. Carrie pulled the pillows beneath the covers to keep warm, holding them tight against her chest and between her feet. Half-asleep, she shivered slightly, unaware if she were freezing to death or had a fever from her accident. She didn't seem to care and didn't have the strength to put the few remaining logs in the stove.

Her leg throbbed with pain, a pain that now seemed distant, almost to belong to someone else. Thoughts and images came and went in black and white. Bart appeared as he had that first night she had met him, clean-shaven, patient and understanding, and full of health and life. He smiled his perfect smile when she asked how he'd been and answered simply, "Fine, and you?" and she poured out how much she missed him when her step-father took her hand and slid it down the front of his trousers and whispered, "Want to see it, honey? Want to?" and she struggled to warm herself and pulled the pillow tighter against her while Mrs. Jenoff and Jake Hornbeck sat at her kitchen counter in La Jolla talking about something she didn't think she was supposed to hear. Finally, she said, "I've made up my mind, Jake. I'm calling 911," and he reached for her and said, "No, cops," and slapped a hand over her mouth and pressed a pillow over her face. She twisted and turned under him and pushed the pillow from her and jammed her hands and forearms between her legs and felt the blankets and the caribou skins being pulled from her in the dark and called out, "Jake, is that you?" and said a prayer that it wasn't when she heard a voice say, "What the hell is going on?" and felt the cold of the cabin rush over her as someone pulled the covers from her. She paused a second to gain her strength and screamed, "This time I will call the cops!" and the voice said, "Take it easy, Carrie, it's okay. It's me. Feather."

"Feather?" Carrie curled in a ball to warm herself, too weak to draw the dark image of her friend to her. "Feather, Feather, Feather," she said, and began to sob. "Thank God you've come."

Feather sat and wrapped her arms around Carrie's huddled form. "Whoa!" she said. "You're half-frozen. You need some warming and in a hurry." She fumbled for the matches in the dark and lit the lantern above the bed. She looked first at Carrie, blue-lipped and shivering, struggling to get beneath her covers, her leg wrapped in a blood-stained tee-shirt, and then at the piles of clothes and vomit on the floor. "What the hell happened?"

Carrie forced out, "I had an accident."

"You sure as shit did."

Feather set the fire and slowly it warmed the cabin and began to bring things back to life for Carrie. Feather sat on the bed, her dark, wide-set eyes narrowing. "Where's Bart?"

"He's not here." Carrie hesitated; she didn't know how to tell her. "He disappeared."

"He *what?*"

Carrie tucked the covers more tightly about her. "He went hunting about a month ago and never came home."

"Just disappeared?"

Carrie began to cry. "I thought I heard a shot, but there was a horrible storm and I couldn't find any tracks or anything."

"A shot? I can't believe it."

A single tear ran down each of Feather's broad, wind-burned cheeks. She turned from Carrie and quickly wiped them away. "It's not like Bart. He could survive anything." She patted Carrie's huddled form. "And after he'd finally found the girl he'd been hoping for."

"You think so?" Carrie said.

"Honest injun," Feather said and both women forced a laugh. "I could tell from the look in his eyes the morning I…" She ran her hands over her thick black hair and looked about the cabin. "No matter. He was a really good man." She turned again to Carrie. "And what happened to you?"

"I hit myself with the axe."

Feather lifted the blankets and looked at Carrie's wound. "How long ago?"

"Yesterday. Today. I'm not sure. I've kind of lost track of time."

"You need to get warmed up and cleaned up." She pulled the covers back over Carrie. "And when was the last time you had something to eat? You're skinny as hell."

"Before my accident, but there's not much food. Bart took the rifle."

"Damn, sister, but you're a mess." Feather stroked Carrie's head. "And you're lucky to be alive."

ONCE THE SAUNA and water were heated, Feather helped Carrie undress. As she did, Carrie could feel her eyes studying her naked body and turned her back.

"You're really thin," Feather said, "but we'll fix that." She ran a finger across the tattoo on the small of Carrie's back. "What's that for? I admired it when I caught you with Bart."

"God, but that seems so long ago," Carrie said. "It's kind of stupid. I swam the butterfly in college."

"I'll bet you were good. You're a big, strong woman."

"Too big for most men."

"But not too big for Bart, so what else matters?" She poured warm water over Carrie's head and back. "This is no time for modesty," she said. "Let's take a look at your wound."

Carrie crossed her arms across her breasts and turned. Feather knelt in front of her, smoothed soap over her calf and washed it clean. She counted the stitches with her finger and looked up. "That hurt like hell?"

Carrie nodded.

"Well, it looks good to me."

She stood and emptied the pitcher over Carrie's curls and asked how she was feeling.

"Better, now that I'm warm."

"I mean without Bart."

"Empty. Alone. I loved him very much."

"Okay." Feather smiled and handed Carrie a towel. "I'll stay until the breakup, if that would help."

"That would more than help."

AFTER THEY'D FINISHED their supper and Feather had emptied her pack, she asked, "Which side of the bed was… is yours?"

"The far side," Carrie said.

Feather fed the fire and stripped down to her stained gray long underwear. The smell of wood smoke mixed with the stench of dried sweat filled the cabin. "How long has it been since *you've* had a bath?" Carrie giggled.

"Six months, maybe more," Feather said. "Don't worry, I'll wash tomorrow. Today was your day." She turned off the lantern and nestled beneath the covers. Again her stench wafted over Carrie who turned away, careful not to disturb the covers and let out more odors.

Carrie fluffed her pillow beneath her head and said goodnight.

"I'm glad I'm here," Feather said.

"Because I was in trouble?" Carrie asked.

"Uh-uh. Because it's the first real bed I've slept in, in months."

Carrie giggled. "You're a piece of work."

"That's what Bart always said."

"As usual, he got it right."

"As usual," Feather said.

The cabin was quiet except for the sound of the logs crackling in the woodstove and the howls of the wolf and his pups.

"What happened to your husky?" Feather asked.

"She got knocked up by a wolf and ran off."

"Shit happens," Feather laughed. "That them calling out there?"

"I'd like to think so," Carrie said.

A gust of wind whistled by the cabin.

"Carrie?"

"Yes."

"I saw that log in the snow. It looks like the beginning of a totem."

"It was Bart's idea."

"If it's okay with you, I'd like to take it up where he left off."

"That would be great." Carrie said.

The logs crackled loudly.

"Carrie?" She felt Feather's hand on her hip, much like the way Bart used to reach for her. "Would it be okay with you if I added myself to the totem?"

Carrie took Feather's hand and squeezed it. "I'd like that. A lot."

Feather rolled away from her and said good night.

"Good night," Carrie said. "Sleep tight."

"You too, sister."

They lay still, Carrie smiling in the dark, the howling of the wolf pack occasionally breaking the silence. Throughout the night, she returned to her routine of tending the fire and thought how much she liked being called sister—how much she had wanted it to be real for as long as she could remember—while Feather slept soundly until dawn, her gentle breathing a night-long comfort.

17

IN THE MORNING Feather returned from the sauna wearing black ski pants and a white turtle neck, her dark, wind-burned skin giving her a look of good health, her wet black hair hanging to her waist. "I feel like a new woman," she said. She raised the cup of coffee that Carrie reached to her in a salute. "Here's to happier times."

Carrie smiled. "That's for sure," she said and headed to the outhouse. As a matter of routine she checked the thermometer: ten degrees Fahrenheit. Tee shirt weather! She stretched her arms and faced the sun, glad to have Feather's companionship, glad to have each day getting longer and warmer. Glad to be alive.

She limped to the outhouse when a wave of nausea swept over her. She stopped, placed her hands on her knees and vomited in the snow. Was she doing too much too soon? What choice did she have? She had to pee, for God's sake. She stayed bent over and waited for the nausea to pass. She wiped her mouth and nose with her mitten, kicked snow over her vomit, and continued to limp to the outhouse. As she pulled the narrow door shut she heard the caw of the raven as it circled high overhead. "Quiet, please," she said in a weak voice. "Can't you see I don't feel well?"

On her way back to the cabin she dropped to all fours and vomited again, her sunglasses falling from her cap into the snow. As she fought the nausea and dizziness and struggled to get her bearings, Feather opened the cabin door and called, "You okay?"

Carrie stood and signaled with a tentative wave that she was all right. She staggered to the cabin, pulled off her parka and cap and collapsed on the bed. "I'm a bit woozy, that's all. Maybe I'm trying to get back to normal too quickly."

"Tea?" Feather said.

Carrie nodded and stared blankly about the cabin.

"Sugar?"

"Please."

Feather handed Carrie her tea and stood over her. "Missed your period?"

Carrie looked at her as though she were trying to bring her into focus. "Oh, my God! I've been so caught up with…" She stood and turned in a circle, tugging at her long blonde curls with her free hand. Bart had told her that the jury was still out about him being able to have kids, and she had said, with so much hope at the time: "So the odds are fifty-fifty."

"I take it the answer is 'yes,'" Feather said.

Carrie placed her hands flat on the table to steady herself and sat. "This is the first time I've been sick."

Feather laid her brown, short-fingered hands over Carrie's. "How do you feel?"

"A little better."

Feather shook her head. "That's not what I'm asking. You happy or sad?"

"Happy. Happy for sure. I was hoping it would happen, but it's so unexpected. I wanted to surprise him if I could."

She smiled. "I thought it would make him finally feel whole; settle his searching, and mine, too."

"He didn't know you were trying?"

Carrie shook her head.

Feather held tight to her hands. "It would have made him very happy."

Carrie squeezed Feather's hands hard. "I hope so." She looked up and kissed Feather. "You're like a gift from heaven."

"Up here you take what you can get," Feather said and pulled on her parka. "And right now this gift's going to split some firewood."

Carrie reached for Feather's hand again. "How would you feel if you were me?"

Feather chuckled. "Think about it, sister. What better gift could he have left you?" She raised her hand as if she weren't really expecting an answer and stepped out the door.

Carrie sipped her tea and stared at the flames in the wood-stove as they weaved back and forth. She thought about her mother and Hannah, and what they would say. She thought about Lola's delivery of her beautiful pups and about what Feather had said when she'd told her that Lola had gotten pregnant by a wolf and run off with him: shit happens.

Well, shit had happened to her; some good, some very, very good; some bad, some very, very bad.

She straightened in her chair as a shadow passed across the window and the raven settled on the snow-covered sill, the feathers on his back and head shining a metallic black in the morning sunlight. He held Carrie's sunglasses in his thick beak and stepped from foot to foot as though he were trying to keep his balance. She patted the top of her curls to feel for her glasses and then stared at the raven in disbelief. For a moment, neither Carrie nor the bird moved, then the raven lowered his head and set the sunglasses on the sill, blinked his good eye at her and with one powerful pump of his wings pushed off and away.

"Jesus," Carrie said. "You know I'm pregnant, too?" She laughed aloud, took a deep breath and the last sip of her tea, and smiled. She was going to have Bart's child and didn't care if the whole world knew it.

18

STANDING HIP TO HIP as they prepared their supper, Carrie raised her cup of tea and tapped it against Feather's. "Here's to warmer, brighter days." She paused and smiled. "And to motherhood."

Feather held her cup against Carrie's. "To motherhood. We'll see about warmer, brighter days. They come with mosquitoes, you know." She returned to stirring the pot in front of her. "We're not going to last more than a few weeks with the food we've got, so tomorrow we'll hunt up some fresh meat."

"*We* will?" Carrie asked.

"For sure," Feather answered.

A LITTLE BEFORE FIVE Feather shook Carrie by the shoulder to wake her. "Up and at it. We need to be at the south meadow before sun-up."

Carrie grunted and pulled the blankets over her head. Feather flipped the blankets and the caribou skins to the foot of the bed and patted the soles of Carrie's wool socks. "Come on. You want to starve to death?"

Carrie stretched, rolled out of bed and stoked the fire, and they dressed in silence. Feather took her rifle from behind the door. "Bart teach you how to use one of these?"

Carrie said he had but that she'd only shot at cans and didn't don't know if she could do this, that she'd never wanted to hurt anything. But before she could tell Feather that she was uncomfortable with what she was being asked to do, Feather loaded the rifle and said they'd better get going, that it would be light before they knew it.

Both hurriedly finished their coffees and stepped outside. By the light of the open cabin door Carrie checked the thermometer while Feather stooped to adjust her snowshoes and mumbled, "Eight above."

"Exactly," Carrie said. "How do you do that?"

"Comes with the territory," Feather said.

They snowshoed to the edge of the woods where Feather put up a gloved-hand and stopped. "Quiet now," she whispered, and handed the rifle to Carrie. "Quiet, and no sudden movements. If we're lucky, we'll get a Sitka." She laid a hand on Carrie's shoulder. "All set?" When she didn't answer, Feather cocked her head and gave her a quizzical look. "You okay?"

Carrie swallowed and nodded.

Feather put a finger to her lips and began to creep through the woods. Carrie followed, stepping where Feather stepped, wondering why each of her steps seemed to make so much noise when Feather's were silent; wondering how Feather could see to avoid brushing the low-hanging branches in the pitch black, knowing that if she asked, all Feather would tell her was that it "came with the territory."

At the border of the large meadow, Feather stopped and beckoned to Carrie to stand by her and motioned for her to lever a round into the chamber. "Now, we wait," she whispered.

A DULL LIGHT began to bathe the snowfield and a chill ran down Carrie's spine. Maybe this was where Bart had hunted. She turned to tell Feather that she couldn't go through with this, that she wanted to leave this place, when a distant group of dark forms moved and came into brighter focus and Feather grabbed the sleeve of her parka and made a sharp gesture with her hand to signal her to be still.

The caribou moved in a slow, halting line, blowing clouds of steam through their large nostrils. Occasionally they pawed heavily with their hooves to find lichen beneath the snow and then lowered their antlered heads to feed. Again Carrie looked pleadingly at Feather, who waggled her index finger at her and, with a small wave of her hand, led Carrie's gaze to the edge of the meadow. Fifty yards to their right, three deer—a buck, a doe, and a fawn—stood motionless, their heads lifted, their ears cocked, wary of the caribou.

Feather mouthed, "Shoot the buck."

A moment passed but Carrie didn't move.

The doe and her fawn remained motionless, never taking their eyes from the caribou but the buck stepped further into the open and turned his head giving Carrie a good look at his widely branched antlers and his broad, brownish gray back. She thought he was so strong-looking, so majestic. How could she shoot something as handsome as that and take him away from his family the way Bart was taken from his.

Feather leaned toward her and raised her mouth to her ear. "Go on. Shoot."

Carrie obediently raised the rifle to her shoulder. Her heart pumped in hard, loud beats; her hands trembled. She heard Bart's calming voice: "Cock, aim and squeeze." She pulled back on the hammer and tried to line up the rifle's sights low on the buck's body behind its shoulder but the rifle jumped in her hands. She took a deep breath to settle herself. She tried aiming again, but it was no use. She couldn't kill anything, especially something that beautiful. She eased the hammer down and lowered the rifle to her waist and turned to Feather and shook her head.

"It's okay," Feather whispered and took the rifle from her.

Carrie squeezed her eyes shut, grimaced and waited. She flinched at the rifle's report and then looked to see what had happened. The buck lay motionless, a spine of one antler protruding above the snow. The doe and her fawn stretched their necks and looked directly at her, their large brown eyes bright in the early daylight, and then wheeled, their bobbing white flags the last Carrie saw of them as they disappeared into the woods.

Feather smiled. "No more Chunky Soup for a while, and no more dog food. That's for sure."

"I'm sorry," Carrie said. "I thought maybe I could do it, but all of a sudden I got very bad vibes about being here."

Feather nodded her head knowingly. "It's okay." She pinned Carrie's arm hard against her. "Some can, some can't."

The two women held tight to one another and snow-shoed toward the buck when the tip of Carrie's snowshoe caught on something buried in the snow and she fell, pulling

Feather off her feet with her. They rolled on their backs and lay in the snow laughing with relief; relief that they were new-found friends and could harvest enough to eat until the breakup. They listened to the raven's incessant cawing from high above the trees and watched as he soared effortlessly above them.

"Do you ever wish you could do that?" Carrie asked. "Just float above everything and not be bothered by all our stupid problems; be kind-of gravity free?"

"Someday you will, and so will I," Feather said and rolled to her knees. "But right now we've got a deer to dress."

"Okeydokey," Carrie said and began to stand but paused and swept at the snow in front of her. She turned to Feather, her eyes wide with fear. "What's this?"

Feather dug in the snow and lifted a rifle from it.

"Oh, my God," Carrie gasped.

Feather pulled her to her feet and handed her the rifle. "You stand there. I'll do the rest." She knelt and began to clear the snow. In a moment her hands stopped moving and she looked up at Carrie and asked, "You ready for this?"

Carrie took a step back and placed her hands on her cheeks. She felt her tears begin to build.

"Okay. Hold tight," Feather said and continued to clear the snow.

Bart lay on his back, his eyes staring at the heavens. Carrie thought he looked so peaceful; so beautiful. She knelt and placed a hand on his cheek. "So he didn't run away?"

"You thought that's what happened?" Feather said.

"I thought maybe I'd asked him to change too much."

"I doubt that," Feather said. She ran her hands over Bart's parka, pulled off his wool cap, inspected his head and brushed the snow from his chest and legs. "Shit!" She looked up at Carrie. "Lola the fucking grizzly queen and her fucking traps. Look."

The snow beneath Bart's right leg was frozen solid with blood, his pant leg and long johns torn, his heavy boot turned grotesquely backward. Feather dug at the snow some more and pulled a snow shoe and a heavy steel trap from it. "He stepped in the trap and either bled or froze to death, or both. Let me see his rifle for a moment." Carrie handed her the carbine and Feather worked its lever, ejecting an empty shell. "That's the shot you thought you heard. It was his signal for help."

Carrie knelt and wrapped her arms around Bart's neck and pressed her cheek against his, his skin and beard cold and hard as ice. She held him briefly, looked away from the blank stare of his large gray eyes and forced herself to look back at him and smoothed his eyelids shut with her bare hand. She kissed his cheek. "I'm going to have your baby. You saved my life. Made it all worth it. Gave me something to live for."

Carrie felt Feather's hand on her shoulder. "I know it's tough, but we've got to take care of business. It's going to get dark in a hurry so go get the dog sled while I clean the deer and then we'll all go home."

ONCE BACK at their campsite, Feather pulled the sled to the foot of a hemlock tree and said, "While I butcher the deer, why don't you take care of Bart?"

Carrie took a tarpaulin from the wood pile beside the cabin and spread it next to the sled and carefully rolled Bart onto it. As she did, the raven settled on his familiar perch in the cottonwood tree. "He's back," she said in a low voice so Feather couldn't hear her. "Is what I'm doing okay?"

The raven stretched his neck, blinked once and pulled his head between his shoulders.

"I'll assume that was a 'yes,'" she said and knelt beside Bart and looked to the darkening sky above Mount Logan and prayed. "Dear God, thank you for the time we've had together and all that he taught me. Thank you for sending me a man I could love and one who could love me. And thank you for giving me his child. And for bringing me here. Please be as gentle with him as he's been with me." She paused. "And, please, help me through this. Help me make it home, to my mother and my friend." She paused and whispered, "I'll love him forever. Amen."

She covered his folded hands with hers and recited the Lord's Prayer. When she was finished, she said, "I'm sorry, Bart, but I can't think what else to do or say."

She kissed his frozen lips, her warm tears staining his face and, as she folded the tarpaulin over him, the line from "The Cremation of Sam McGee" haunted her: *Yet 'tain't being dead—it's my awful dread of the icy grave that pains…*and Carrie shook her head. "I'm sorry, gorgeous adventurer," she sobbed, "but it's the best I can do."

19

WITH BART'S MYSTERY finally solved, for the first time since he'd disappeared Carrie was at peace with herself. She constantly dreamed about the moment she could leave, checking off the days on the calendar and watching—with wonderment mixed with impatience—as the red February sun turned a warming yellow, the first marking that spring was on its way. She thought it must be Alaska's natural traffic light; when the snow disappeared and the meadows showed green it would be time to go. Time to head home.

She tore the page for March from the calendar and crumpled it into a ball and threw it in the woodstove and thought things were looking up. She re-hung the calendar above the stove and ran a finger under April and smiled, for each day was now filled with encouragement that life was blooming all about her, not to mention the life she was now carrying which was stirring with a new vitality. Her nausea had all but disappeared and, although the scar on her calf was an ugly, jagged reminder of her accident, her wound had healed without an infection.

While Feather carved the totem, Carrie began to take longer and longer snowshoe treks as though she were trying to imprint her wilderness experience deep into her soul in case she never returned. On her outings she paused in the meadows and watched the caribou herds push north to their calving grounds and studied the Dall sheep as they moved sure-footedly over the rocky mountain terrain, white against the melting landscape; the rams with their brown, full-curled horns, the ewes smaller and round-bellied, carrying their lambs. The thought that these animals were soon to give birth caused her to smile and smooth her hand over her own belly, for she expected her child to begin to show soon.

On more than one occasion she paused near a stand of willows and watched moose, with their spindly legs and heavy bodies and heads, break the willow branches and chew the still hidden buds at their tips. It was here that she first noticed the paw prints and yellow-brown piscicles in the snow left by Lola and her pups and thought Thelma and Louise and their five brothers must be growing up just fine.

But all these comforting experiences were bittersweet, for with each came a vacantness and sorrow, as Carrie thought how much Bart would have enjoyed them and how much she would have loved to share them with him.

MIDMONTH, while Carrie was preparing two small venison steaks for supper, Feather waved to her through the window and called, "Come look at what I've done."

Carrie hurried to Feather's side and studied the cedar log that lay in the wet snow and stuttered, "I'm...I'm...I'm speechless."

The bottom four feet of the log were untouched; Bart had said it would be placed in the ground to hold the totem securely in place. The first figure, square-headed and flat-faced, held a salmon to its chest. It was Bart's self-portrait, and while he joked he always knew he'd end up low man on the totem pole, he'd also emphasized that this figure, and the one above it, were the foundations for the family they supported.

The next figure—Bart's rendering of Carrie—was tall, its face surrounded by curly hair, the curls framing a straight row of teeth and thick lips that turned upward at their edge.

Sitting on Carrie's curls were seven miniature animal-like figures with a larger animal above them that featured a long nose and drooping teats. They were a tribute to Lola and her pups and the last renderings Bart had carved.

Above Lola, Feather had carved a wolf with a wide rectangular mouth of jagged teeth and a pair of almond-shaped eyes. On top of the wolf was Feather herself, a small figure with pigtails clutching an infant at her breast.

A raven stood erect at the top of the totem, its wings tight against its sides, the curve of its thick beak giving it a sour look. It stared up from the snow at Carrie with one eye, the other nothing more than a slash-mark from Feather's hatchet.

Carrie turned to her and wrapped her arms around her. "It's perfect," she sobbed. "It's our whole story and it includes you."

"Holding your baby," Feather said, "as your sister. So our bond will never be broken."

After supper, Feather took Carrie by the hand and sat with her at the foot of the bed. "Listen," she said. "Tomorrow we put up our totem." Carrie felt Feather's hand tighten. "And take care of Bart."

"Take care of him?"

"It's time," Feather said. "The thaw's here and we can't wait any longer. But don't worry, we'll do it right. I've prepared his sacred place."

Carrie looked down and rubbed her feet across the caribou skin on the floor. "The totem and burying him are kind of like the final act," she said. "Right?" She paused and continued to stare at the floor, then looked up at Feather. Her eyes filled with tears. "It's over, isn't it?"

"In a way," Feather said. "In other ways, it's just beginning."

THE SUN began to warm the cabin when Feather rolled beneath the blankets and tapped Carrie on the arm. "Time to get up. We've got work to do."

Carrie sat and uttered a loud yawn. She stretched her arms above her head, yawned again and flipped her long curls over her shoulders. "How about the totem and a haircut and that's it?"

Feather shook her head. "Not today. Besides, putting it off won't make it any easier."

"For me or for you?" Carrie said and wrapped her arms across her stomach and rocked forward and back. "I once asked Bart if he loved you, but I've never asked if you loved him."

For a moment, Feather cupped her hands over her ears, then slowly drew them away. "What'd he say?"

"That's not the point," Carrie said.

Feather stared at the ceiling. "Got it, but first, what did *he* say?"

"That you were too much alike; that you had the wanderlust."

"That's it?" Feather said.

"No. He said you were his friend, that if you liked someone, you'd be the best friend they ever had."

"That's all?"

"You were hoping for something more?" Carrie paused. "Oh my God, you *were* in love with him."

Feather threw off the covers and swung her feet to the floor. "Enough of this white man's talk. We've got work to do."

"Feather!" Carrie said. "What kind of talk is that?"

Feather rested her head in her hands, her thick black hair falling over her face. "Of course I loved him. But it never could have worked. We were earths apart." She massaged her temples as if in pain. "You're the one he loved and now here we are, both abandoned by him. Me for a second time. You with his child. Two young widows about to bury the man they loved. Not exactly what dreams are made of, but it is what it is and it's up to us to do it right."

Carrie stared at the small dark woman in red flannel underwear who sat at the edge of her bed, now visibly trying to control her sobbing, a stranger who had become her friend when she needed a friend the most. "I know it's not what you want to hear," she began.

"Then don't say it," Feather snapped.

"But we *will* do it right," Carrie said.

"Good."

"And, Feather, for what it's worth, *I* love you."

"I know you do," Feather said. "Now, let's get to work."

Carrie laughed and once again thought, up here you take what you can get.

THEY TOOK TURNS digging and by noon they had dug a hole at the edge of the clearing and set the totem in it, the crudely carved figures facing the cabin so they could be admired from the window. Carrie rested her chin on the top of the shovel handle while Feather wiped snow and mud from the knees of her pants. "We're all there," Carrie said. "Just the way it ought to be."

Feather looked up at her and smiled. "Now comes the hard part." She signaled to Carrie to follow her and they wandered into the woods until Feather stopped at a stand of birches that bordered a narrow stream. She pointed to a platform of cedar logs that reached between the white branches of one birch to the branches of another and then walked to the platform and ran a hand over their reddish-brown bark. "While you were out snow-shoeing I built this for Bart. This is his resting place. Once we set him here, this becomes a sacred burial ground that only you and I—and someday your baby—can visit."

Carrie looked about her. The sun shone through the trees, its light scattered across the snow-patched forest floor. She was pleased by the site but confused. "Don't we bury him in a grave? You know, in a hole?"

"No," Feather said. "Here his spirit will be close to all the things he loved—the mountains, the forest, the streams, the howl of the wolves, the stars."

All the things that Carrie had grown to love too. "It's perfect." She smiled. "Just the way he'd want it. He'll be happy here." She slipped her arm through Feather's. "I'd like to do it now. It will help put things in order. The way Bart would want them."

"Okay, sister," Feather said, "let's go get him."

20

JAKE HORNBECK SAT on the steps of the one-room building at the McCarthy airstrip rubbing insect repellant over his hands, neck, face and ears while he watched a blue and gold airplane curl into a sharp turn and begin its final approach. For an instant the plane seemed to stall over the far end of the dirt runway as the growl of its engine was cut back to a muffled whir, then its front wheels bounced twice before the plane settled on its tail wheel and slowed to a stop. Jake waved a mosquito away from his ear and thought this must be his backwoods meal ticket and turned the ID tags on his large-frame pack and aluminum rifle case so that the name Johnny Archer, written in large, bold print, could be read at a distance. He straightened and waited while the pilot freed his potbellied frame from the cockpit and kicked large yellow chocks beneath the plane's wheels.

"Johnny Archer?" the pilot said.

"You got it," Jake said.

The pilot studied him for a moment and fumbled in a pocket of his red-and-black-checked shirt for his cigarettes. He lit one and put out his hand. "Welcome to McCarthy, where the road ends and the wilderness begins."

What a crock of horseshit, Jake thought. "You must be Whitey Hurd."

"Since birth," Whitey said, and then added, "Man, you're red on the head like stink on shit."

Jake ran his hand over his once-straight black hair now dyed an orange-red. "Since birth," he answered, satisfied that his new appearance had already impressed this man who was to be his unwitting accomplice.

"Say, that's a good one." Whitey chuckled. "We're even." He pointed towards Jake's pack and rifle case. "That's all your gear?"

"It's all I need," Jake said.

Whitey dragged on his cigarette. "For how long?"

"A week, but there's enough there to last me a month."

"No shit?" Whitey said. "You've done this before?"

Jake pressed his lips together and nodded. "Plenty of times, in plenty of places."

"Those places include Alaska?"

Jake shook his head. "You've seen one, you've seen 'em all."

Whitey raised his eyebrows and blew smoke through his mouth and nose. "You may find Alaska a bit different."

Jake waived a hand in front of his face to keep the smoke away.

Whitey didn't seem to notice and asked, "What is it, exactly, that you plan to do?"

Jake wanted to tell him that was none of his fucking business, but he didn't want any trouble. He needed to enlist this man's help and knew he must keep his cool and reinforce his new identity. "Get away from the hassle of Seattle," he said. "You know, after a while, the city drives me nuts—"

"I don't know, but I'll take your word for it," Whitey said.

Jake was determined to finish what he had planned to say. It was an important part of his plan. "A friend of mine told me there's good camping near the Wrangell Mountain Expeditions Camp."

Whitey laughed. "*Where* near the Wrangell Mountain camp? You've only got thirteen million acres to choose from."

Jake felt himself beginning to anger. He took a deep breath and pushed his hands in the pockets of his hiking pants. "I'm not really sure, Captain, but this is a team effort. I'm going to need your help on some of this."

"It's your money," Whitey said, "and I'll do whatever I can to help. It's two-fifty in and two-fifty out. Cash on the barrelhead." He took a drag on his cigarette and extended an open hand. "I'll take it all up front, if you don't mind."

"Who's to say you'll come back for me when it's time?" Jake asked.

"I'm a man of my word, city boy," Whitey said. "That's one of the things I mean about it being a bit different up here. We mean what we say and say what we mean. Me? I work for money, and I'll do anything to get it, as long as it's on the up and up."

Jake stared at Whitey. He didn't like being called "city boy" or being lectured, but took comfort that his ruse was working.

Whitey beckoned with the fingers of his open hand. "All or nothing," he said. "And you can bet your life I'll be back to get you, as long as the weather cooperates."

Jake pulled a thick roll of bills from his pocket. Whitey whistled at the sight of the money. "How much you got there? Five, ten thousand?"

Jake shook his head and peeled off five one hundred dollar bills. "There's more where that came from if all goes well."

"Don't worry, I'll hold up my end of the bargain." Whitey took the money, folded it neatly and stuffed it in his shirt pocket. "Okay, city boy, let's go flying."

"Johnny," Jake said through clenched teeth. "Johnny Archer."

"Whatever," Whitey said, reaching for the door of the small building. "Take your gear to the Cub. I'll check in and then we're good to go."

ONCE JAKE'S PACK and rifle were stowed and Whitey and he were settled in the cramped aircraft, they flew over Sourdough Peak and then south to the Chitina River and followed it southeast. "The river's getting ready to break up. Should happen any day now," Whitey said through his headset. He pointed to his right. "That's the Bremner gold mine at about two o'clock. It's been abandoned for sixty years. The next sign of civilization, if you can call it that, will be the Wrangell Camp."

"Anybody live out here?" Jake asked.

"Just a guy named McFee from California and his yearly something or other."

Bingo! Jake tried to sound curious but not too interested. "A yearly something or other?"

"Yeah. McFee brings a different woman with him every winter to keep him company. None of them ever come back. It's a crazy stunt, but the women keep falling for it. They all say he's got something you and I don't."

Jake thought, we'll see, and sat in silence, drumming on his thighs with open hands, his plan now definitely falling into place.

"That's the Wrangell Camp straight ahead," Whitey said.

"Good," Jake grunted. "Can you show me where these crazy women live?"

Whitey laughed. "Okay, but don't get your hopes up. There's only one a year and I don't think McFee's much into sharing."

Jake watched as the arrow on the altimeter slowly rotated past two thousand feet to fifteen hundred. He stared at the trees and meadows below him. As the plane droned on he thought he'd never seen wilderness like this before, could never have imagined anything could be so vast, so beautiful. Finally his thoughts were interrupted by the pilot saying, "Look to your left."

In the distance Jake could make out hundreds, perhaps thousands, of animals inching across the tundra.

"That's one big herd of caribou," Whitey said and banked the plane. "Okay, McFee's cabin is coming up in the clearing on the right. Keep an eye out, there's not much to it." In a moment he tapped the windshield. "There you are. Home sweet home."

Jake stared at the two small cabins. Carrie had dumped him for that? "Some guy lives in that? All winter?"

"Until the breakup," Whitey said and circled above the camp site.

"And he doesn't freeze to death?"

Whitey put the plane into a climb and headed west. "Not a chance. He's a different sort of guy, but he sure as hell knows what he's doing in the bush. No one would argue that." Whitey chuckled. "And he cuts one hell of a lot of fire wood."

"Huh," Jake said as though he wasn't interested and asked, "How far to a good camping site?"

"I can set you down three or four miles from here. You'll have some open water and some damn good views of Mount Logan."

"Let's do it," Jake said.

Whitey leaned forward in his seat; looked hard left and then hard right. "Okay, here we go." He banked toward a green strip of meadow and set the plane down and rolled it to a stop. "Smooth as a gravy sandwich." He laughed and switched off the engine. "Well, Mr. Archer, welcome to the end of the line."

He unloaded Jake's gear and carried it a distance from the plane where Jake opened the aluminum case, took out the rifle and leaned it against his pack.

"You planning on shooting an elephant?" Whitey asked.

Jake latched the case closed and handed it to the pilot. "Just wanted to be ready for anything."

"The real question is, can you hit *anything* with that big son of a bitch?"

Jake nodded. "I'm fine. Just fine, thank you."

They walked back to the plane where Whitey stowed the rifle case and opened the door to the cockpit.

"See you here in a week?" Jake said. "Seven days. Guaranteed?"

"Don't worry, I'll be here." Whitey stood in front of the plane's open door for a minute and then said, "Listen, Johnny, are you sure you can take care of yourself out here? This isn't exactly Seattle, you know."

"What makes you think I can't?"

"Just a hunch. I don't want to see you get in over your head."

"Well, hunch this," Jake said and grabbed Whitey by the front of his shirt and lifted him off his feet and set him on the edge of the pilot's seat. "Not bad for a city boy, huh?"

Whitey whistled through his teeth. "Well, don't that beat all. I guess you're going to be okay after all."

Jake stepped away from the plane and raised a hand to his red eyebrow and saluted and smiled. He had finally gotten the better of Whitey and sensed his plan was working well. Very well indeed. "You're fucking A I'll be okay, Captain. See you in a week, and don't be late."

"A week it is," Whitey said. "You can bet your life on it."

A HALF-MILE from McFee's cabin Jake stopped walking and sat on his bulging backpack. He watched the sun make its silent exit behind the mountains, the open space in front of him turning to purple and then to black. Nightfall quieted all around him and a pinpoint of a light appeared in the distance. He smiled for he knew a lantern had been lit in the McFee cabin. Right on cue, you clueless assholes, he thought, and wished Bart and Carrie a nice night. And that asshole pilot didn't think he was ready for this? He laughed aloud. He'd show him; just the way he'd showed that mouthy Jenoff bitch, snuffing her without a clue and Carrie's whereabouts stuck big as life on her refrigerator door. Clueless assholes! None of them knew who they were dealing with. But just the same, he chided himself with his constant refrain of no more fuck-ups; no more lapses in discipline. No more, Jake, old buddy. No more.

With these thoughts he laid his arms across his knees and rested his forehead on the sleeve of his fleece and closed his eyes. He tried to visualize all he planned to do, going through his mental checklist one last time. Satisfied that there wouldn't be any stupid last-minute mistakes, he stood, worked his arms through the straps of his pack and hunched it onto his back and checked his rifle to see that a round was in the chamber.

And then he began.

He crept into the woods, intent upon circling the cabin, and kept the comforting light at his left shoulder and visible at all times. In the distance he heard a howl that sent a shiver down his spine. He stopped and took a deep breath. Make the night your friend, he ordered himself. Make it work for you. In a moment he heard the howl again. The thought that there were wolves on the prowl this night pleased him, and he started through the woods now thinking he was one of them.

He picked his way along a low ridge, his path illuminated from time to time by a half-moon that shone from behind drifting clouds. When he was opposite the cabin, he turned down a hillside to a small opening where he stopped and waited for a cloud to finish covering the moon. He thought he was close enough to the cabin and needed a place to sleep. He listened to the sound of running water and, when the cloud cleared the moonlight's path, he could see the inky reflection of a stream in front of him. He thought this would be as good a spot as any when he noticed a dense black object hanging in the trees on the other side of the stream. He stepped on the dark stones that protruded from the water and walked toward the object to satisfy his curiosity, the tree trunks and branches of a stand of birches now showing a ghostly white in the full moonlight.

He stared at the form suspended between the trees but still couldn't make out what it was. He hesitated a moment and thought if he was careful his light couldn't be seen. He pulled a thin flashlight from a nylon sheath on his belt, pointed it at the dark form and twisted the light on.

He gasped and took a step back. "What the fuck?" He shuddered and moved the light's beam up and down the corpse several times and then trained it on its gray face. It was McFee. At least he guessed it was. He had only seen him once, during their brief encounter in La Jolla, and the man who had challenged him that night was clean shaven while the face in front of him that grew brighter as the light of the moon flooded over it was covered by a dark beard. It had to be him. Jake chuckled. So the hippie pussy was dead. Perfect. One less problem for him to deal with. Something or someone saved him a bullet and Carrie would be all alone. "Perfect," he whispered. "Better than I could expect. She might even welcome the company."

He turned off his light. "Well, ashes to ashes and all that good shit," he said and reached across McFee and grabbed him by the shoulder of his jacket to pull him to the ground when he heard a growl behind him.

And then another.

And another.

He loosened his grip on McFee's jacket and turned and inched the rifle from his shoulder and eased it to his waist and pushed the safety off. He heard a twig snap and thought he saw something move in the blackness. He twisted the flashlight on and, holding it against the rifle, turned it with the weapon, sweeping its narrow beam in the direction of the growling. At first the light illuminated a tuft of grass, then bounced about the rotted stump of a tree, then over a patch of snow. Jake continued to search to his left, suddenly stopping the light on two almond-shaped yellow eyes no more than thirty yards from him. "Stay where you are, you big son of a bitch." He didn't want to have to shoot, to alert Carrie that he was there.

The wolf growled, lifted a paw and stepped toward him. Jake raised the rifle to his shoulder. "Stay where you are," he said again. "You're fucking up my plan."

As he spoke, he heard another growl. He swept the rifle and the flashlight further to his left until the beam shone on a pair of washed-out blue eyes. Behind them pairs of smaller eyes dotted the darkness like fireflies. Shit, he thought, he hadn't planned on this.

He moved the light and the rifle back to the first animal. Its dark lips were drawn back, its large teeth shining bright white in the beam of the flashlight. The wolf took another step toward him. Jake told himself to waste the son of a bitch. What could Carrie do now? He had her trapped.

He settled the sight's black crosshairs between the yellow eyes and then he heard the animal to his left begin its charge. He swung the rifle, the flashlight slipping from his grip, and fired at the rapidly closing, snarling dark form. For a moment all was black, save for the flashlight lying at his feet, throwing its beam on one of his boots. He chambered another bullet and stooped to retrieve his light, then swept it through the woods, illuminating a number of fleeting, ghost-like forms. He fired another shot out of spite and yelled, "No one fucks with Jake Hornbeck. No one." He worked the bolt once more, slammed it shut and chastised himself to give it a rest, not to lose it now.

21

CARRIE STOOD at the woodstove stirring a pot of soup when she was startled by the faraway report of a rifle. She stopped stirring and glanced at Feather. She had been thinking that she finally had things under control, that the breakup was almost upon them, and soon she'd be on her way home. The echo of a second shot rolled through the valley. "What's going on?" she asked. "That sounds like shots."

"You got it," Feather said.

Carrie moved from the stove to the window and peered into the blackness. "Are you sure?"

Feather took her rifle from behind the door, levered a round into the chamber and lowered the hammer. "Sure I'm sure."

"Then what...?" She stopped as Feather reached over her and lifted Bart's rifle from the nails behind the stove and began to load it. "What are you doing?"

"Playing it safe," Feather said. "It's an odd time of year for some idiot poacher to be out this far."

Carrie went back to stirring the soup, trying to conceal her anxiety. She tasted a small sampling and added some salt. Without looking up, she said, "Could it be trouble?"

"Hard to say." Feather stood the rifles on either side of the bed. "But tonight we bolt the door, just in case."

Carrie hadn't locked a door since leaving California and the thought took her back to Hannah and her apartment and how long ago all that seemed. She sighed and poured soup into two cups and set them on the table. The thought of her apartment made her think of Bill Davies, or Davis, or whatever his name was, but she dismissed the thought with a shake of her head and a muttered, "No."

Feather latched the door and sat at the table. "No? No what?"

"Just thinking the worst and wondering what's going on."

"Me, too," Feather said and sipped her soup and squinted at Carrie as though she were looking for an answer. "I never did ask. Did you come out here to get away from someone?"

Carrie shook her head. The intensity of Feather's look made her feel like a child being confronted by a teacher. "Not really. I came out here to get away from everyone, and everything, and to be with Bart."

"And what about Bart? Was someone looking for him?"

Carrie smiled. "Only me."

Feather tapped the table with her stubby index finger. "This is no time to get sappy on me. Answer up."

"Sorry," Carrie said. "We talked about this type of stuff after you told us Whitey had said someone was trying to reach us and Bart swore no one was after him."

"Sounds like if we're careful, we should be all right," Feather said and patted the seat of the chair next to her the way Bart used to when he wanted to talk. "Now sit and have your meal. You're eating for two, remember?"

CARRIE WOKE the next morning to the rumble of thunder rolling low over the foothills at the base of the mountains. It was the first thunder she'd heard since she'd been in camp and it made her think how much things were changing. She sat, stretched her arms above her head and ran her hands through her long curls and then gently over her belly. Feather was already seated at the table, sipping a cup of tea and reading *Deliverance* by the gray light that shone through the window. Her rifle leaned against the wall within her reach.

"What do you think?" Carrie asked.

Without looking up from her book Feather said, "I think it's going to rain."

"That's not what I meant. Do you think we're okay?"

"I hope so, but take the rifle with you when you pee."

"Really?"

"Really," Feather said, nodding but still not looking up.

Carrie crawled out of bed, pulled her fleece over her nightie, slipped on her boots without lacing them and picked up the rifle. As she stepped out the door, a jagged flash of lightning streaked across the foot of Mt. Logan. She paused and waited for the thunder to follow and looked at her surroundings. The path to the outhouse, now grassy, wet and muddy, was bordered by a dirty wall of snow, a reminder of the winter's daily shoveling, and the trees showed a misty green as their buds made their first showings. It had been almost seven months. In an odd way she missed the cold, the wind and the snow, and what Bart referred to so often as "the damned darkness." These were among the things she would remember most for they had brought Bart and her together and kept them in place until their love for one another had taken over. They were also the enemy she'd had to battle to prove to Bart and to Hannah—and to herself—that she could do it, that she could survive.

She smiled and pumped her hands above her head, one hand tightly clutching the rifle. She had done it. She'd made it, and now it was time to go home. She started toward the outhouse, her smile growing broader with each step. She felt freer than she could ever remember.

On her way back to the cabin the jabbering of the raven startled her, then amused her, as the bird settled on his carved likeness atop the totem with a noisy flapping of his wings. She cocked her head and closed one eye to imitate his familiar pose. "And how are you today my friend?"

"Fine, and how are *you*?" a male voice answered.

Carrie drew in a large breath of air. "Oh, Jesus!" She spun around to see who had spoken to her.

A man with a black baseball cap pulled down over his eyes stepped from behind the outhouse. He raised a rifle to his shoulder and trained it directly on her face. "Drop the gun."

The voice was familiar. It couldn't be, she thought, and then remembered Jake's words: "I'll track you to the ends of the earth to settle this score." She choked out, "Jake?"

"Drop the fucking gun," he said.

"What are you doing here?"

He took a step toward her, the rifle still pointed at her. "I'm here to settle the score, so drop the gun or you'll end up with your hippie friend swinging in a tree."

"You bastard."

"You heard me, Carrie, drop the fucking gun."

She heard the click of the safety as he pushed it forward and laid his cheek along the rifle's comb. She paused for a moment and then let go of the rifle.

"Now back up. Five steps and stop," Jake said.

Carrie's eyes never left him as she silently counted her steps and stopped at five. She thought he looked different somehow, but couldn't put her finger on how.

"Good, now don't move." He walked slowly in her direction and stopped at the totem. "What's this shit all about?" he said and kicked at the pole.

"Don't do that," Carrie said.

He laughed and kicked the totem a second time. "I'm calling the shots here, not you."

"Please, don't do that again. That's mine and …" She stopped. She didn't want to share anything about the totem or what it signified.

Jake stooped to pick up her rifle. As he did, the raven sailed down from the totem, snatched the Seattle Mariners cap from his head and pumped its wings to climb above him.

"What the fuck!" Jake bellowed. He shouldered his rifle, centered the crosshairs on the rising black bird, and fired. The raven faltered and began to fall, his wings tight against his side, the ball cap still in his beak. "Got him!" Jake yelled and watched as the bird's wings fluttered before it collapsed in a patch of snow.

"You bastard," Carrie said again. "He was my friend." With Jake's back to her she tiptoed a few steps toward the cabin and then broke into a run, yelling, "Feather, come quick!"

Jake wheeled and pointed his rifle at her. "Hold it right there."

Carrie stopped and threw her hands above her head in surrender. The cabin door opened slightly and the muzzle of Feather's rifle showed blue-black in the gray morning light.

"Drop it, whoever you are," Jake said, "or I'll kill the bitch on the spot."

The camp was silent. Neither rifle wavered from its target.

Jake took a step to his left to put Carrie between him and his adversary.

Finally, Carrie said, "Do what he says, Feather. Please. I know this guy and he's crazy and he *will* kill me."

"Shit," Feather said. She pushed her weapon through the crack in the door and let it fall into the muddy patch in front of the cabin.

"Good," Jake said. "Now step out here with your two-timing friend so I can see who we've got."

Feather stepped through the door. "Well, I'll be god-damned," Jake said. "A smart Indian. Who would have ever guessed it?" He pointed at the women with his rifle and told them to stand by the wood pile.

Feather didn't move. Instead, she took Carrie by the hand. "You know him?"

Carrie dragged her toward the nearby stack of wood. "He's one of the reasons I left California, but I never thought he'd go this far."

"Bill what's-his-name?" Feather asked.

"No, and I don't know how—"

"Shut the fuck up and don't try anything," Jake said. "Anyone else in the cabin?"

Carrie felt Feather's grip tighten and heard her whisper, "It's okay. We'll find a way."

Carrie looked at Jake for a moment without answering and shook her head. "No."

"You're not fucking with me, are you?"

"She's not fucking with you," Feather said, her voice flat and matter-of-fact. "It's just the two of us."

He picked up the rifles and unloaded them and leaned them against the cabin and peered inside. He looked at Carrie. "Know why I'm here?"

Carrie found it difficult to swallow, let alone talk. All she could do was shake her head. "Jake, please—"

"No please about it. No one dumps Jake Hornbeck for no good reason, especially not for some fucking hippie stranger."

Carrie began to cry. "Please, Jake, just let us alone."

He slipped his pack from his back, rested it at his feet, and squatted and unzipped one of its side pockets and pulled a coil of olive drab nylon cord from it. He stood and gestured toward the cabin door with his rifle's muzzle. "Inside. Now. You and the Indian."

Inside the cabin, Carrie and Feather stood awkwardly by the table, still holding hands. "You spent the winter in this?" Jake said. "What a shit hole!" He pointed to the bed. "Okay, Carrie. Lie down. Face down. Hands behind your head."

Carrie didn't move.

"Have it your way," he said and jammed the rifle's muzzle between her breasts.

Carrie felt Feather squeeze her hand and then let go, and she did as she was told.

"Now, the squaw, on the floor, in the same position, and don't try anything funny."

Feather lay on the floor and Jake tied her ankles together, then told her to put her hands behind her back. He ran the cord around her wrists and drew her feet against her thighs and tied her hands tightly to her feet and laughed. "A hogtied Indian. What a sight."

He tapped Carrie on her foot with the rifle barrel. "Payback time." He laughed again. "Take off that silly outfit and roll over."

Carrie didn't move. Her plea of "Please, Jake, no," was muffled by the pillow near her mouth.

Jake jabbed the rifle's muzzle hard in her ribs. "I'm not here to negotiate. Take off your fucking clothes."

Carrie rolled over, sat and pulled off her fleece.

"Everything," he said.

She took off her boots and socks, stuffed a sock in each boot and set them side by side on the floor. She hesitated, then pulled her nightshirt over her head and folded it neatly and set it on the bed and pulled her knees to her chest and wrapped her arms around them to cover herself.

"Lie back," Jake said and smiled. "Enjoy it, while you can."

Carrie remained hunched over. Tears ran down her cheeks. "No, Jake. Please."

He pressed the cold muzzle of the rifle against her cheek. "Lie back or you eat this."

"Please?"

He shook his head and for the first time Carrie realized what was different about him, and thought that small talk might soften him, might somehow change things. "What have you done to your hair?"

"Shut the fuck up and lie back."

She pleaded again.

Jake pushed the safety off. "Pick your poison."

Slowly Carrie unfolded her body and lay back.

"Smart. Two smart cunts," Jake said. He poked Carrie's pubic hair with the rifle and pushed the muzzle between her legs. "Spread them. Your arms, too."

Carrie closed her eyes and did what she was told.

Jake moved about the bed and tied her wrists and ankles to its frame, holding her spread-eagle. He ran his hand in a circle over her belly. "A little pudgy, but pretty much the way I remembered it." He ran the rifle's muzzle along the scar on her calf and laughed. "McFee do that to you or were you bit by a bear?"

"Bart wasn't like that," she sobbed.

"Pussies rarely are." He rested his rifle on the table, closed the cabin door and bolted it. He took off his fleece, undid his belt and moved to the bed. The sound of the zipper on his fly being pulled down seemed to fill the cabin.

"No!" Feather screamed.

Jake reached down and lifted her so she was facing the bed. "There. Better?" He laughed. "Now you can watch the main event."

"No!" Feather screamed again. "She's pregnant!"

He looked at Feather and then at Carrie. "You're shitting me."

Carrie opened her eyes. "She's telling the truth. I'm going to have a baby." When she said the words they gave her a feeling of satisfaction, of power, but she wasn't sure over what.

"That hippie pussy knocked you up?"

"It's Bart's child, if that's what you mean," Carrie said.

Jake sat at the table, his pants at his knees, and put his head in his hands. A stream of gray light covered his newly reddened hair, his muscular upper body, his tattoos. "I hadn't figured on this." He sighed. Finally, he stood and kicked Feather's thigh. "Well, maybe she'll have twins when I get through with her."

Feather looked up at him, her eyes narrow and filled with anger. "You'll never get away with this."

Jake shrugged and walked to the edge of the bed and grabbed Carrie by her hair and jerked her head from the pillow and pulled her close to him when a shadow fell across the cabin floor. He glanced over his shoulder at the window. A wide-eyed boy with black hair held in place by a red and white bandana stared back at him and then moved away as quickly as he had appeared.

Jake pulled hard on Carrie's hair. "I thought you said we were alone."

"We are," Carrie said.

"Bullshit." He pulled up his pants and began to fasten them. "Who's the Indian kid?"

"What Indian kid?" Feather asked.

Jake bent and slapped her across the face. "Don't play dumb with me." He lifted her by the hair, suspending her from the floor. Blood trickled from the corner of her mouth. "Who is he?"

Feather shook her head, signaling she didn't know or wasn't going to answer. Jake let her fall to the floor and kicked her in the stomach. "Makes no difference to me."

He pulled on his fleece and took his rifle from the table. "Don't you two girls go anywhere. The party's just begun." He laughed a long, high-pitched laugh and unlatched the cabin door and stepped outside into a steady, cold rain.

22

STORYTELLER WHEELED from the cabin window, slipped out of his pack and sprinted to the woods, gripping his bow tightly, his large bowie knife slapping against his thigh with each frantic step. He tried desperately to make sense of what he'd just witnessed for up until now his world had been the natural world where there were no strangers with rifles, no one was trying to harm his sister, no one that didn't belong was in his friend's cabin. There was none of that.

Two days before he had set his small birch bark canoe high on the bank of the frozen Chitina River and tied the frayed painter to an alder, the alder's catkins showing blood red in the noonday sun. He'd laid his small camouflage pack carefully in the canoe and slipped his bandana from his forehead, smoothing his long black hair and retying the red and white cloth as he studied the changing world before him.

Patches of wet grass spread throughout the receding snow. Cottonwoods abandoned their stiff, winter brittleness, the tips of their branches showing the pale green promise of re-growth. Beavers swam in the open water of the shallow ponds and muskrats once again began to dive and disappear in the frigid blackness of the thawing streams. Long-tailed ducks, Mallards, Mergansers, Goldeneyes and Pintails and geese by the thousands flew the rivers' banks searching for food and a spot to rest, a place to breed. Mosquitoes were beginning to bite and would soon swarm so thick they would worry the caribou.

He watched a string of ducks far out over the river turn toward him. He lifted his bow from the canoe, drew an arrow from his small quiver and settled in the alders, peering through their thick branches as the ducks flew silently, silhouetted black against the cloudless blue sky. When they neared the far bank he cupped his hands by his mouth and called for them. The ducks began to circle, flying lower and lower, never slowing their rapid wing beats. Storyteller changed his call from a loud nasal quacking to a rapid choking sound to signal that there were other ducks feeding nearby. His prey swung downriver and turned back into the wind. He made the choking sound once more, notched his arrow on his bowstring and waited.

The birds came to him, their wings set to land. Storyteller waited until two drakes were directly above him, one slightly higher than the other, their metallic green heads flashing in the sun. His arrow passed through the thin white collar on the lower duck's neck and lodged in the ruddy breast of the bird above it. Both birds began to pump their wings to climb from danger, struggled and fell clumsily from the sky.

The boy walked down the muddy river bank no more than a hundred yards and picked up the birds. He pulled the arrow free, wiped its razor-sharp head on his pants and carried his prey upriver. It was time he thought, and perched on the gunwale of his canoe and waited in silence for nature's permission to cross.

He felt it before he heard it.

It began with a shuddering through the soles of his boots that became a guttural rumble as it rolled down river toward him, its roar growing in volume until it drowned out all other sounds. Storyteller looked up and studied the ice groaning and bulging with pressure from beneath. The first crack sounded like a rifle shot as the ice began to break into slabs as large as the logging trucks that roared along the highways, the floes wedging and folding over each other, heaving twenty, then thirty feet high. They moved past him like a thunderous parade of the winter's work, scouring and uprooting alders and bushes from the banks, crushing others in their path, one gray floe carrying two yearling caribou bawling and stepping nervously in place as they rode down river.

The roaring continued until the last sandy, gray ice pans floated by or were shelved awkwardly on the banks. All was followed by silence and the calm flow of the glacial milky-gray water of the Chitina River when a lone tree slipped past, a broken cow moose tangled in its gnarled roots, marking the end of nature's annual review.

The boy stroked his chin, his hand moving over the black sparse beginnings of facial hair, and muttered, "Holy shit." He sat for a moment more and then untied his canoe, dragged it down the bank, slid it into the frigid water and paddled hard against the current to the far shore.

For Storyteller, and all his companions in the wilderness, the breakup signaled the beginning of birth and growth, and encouraged him that good things were soon to come. But all that had changed. Now he was an animal on the run and sensed he would be hunted to the death by the strange man with the red hair in McFee's cabin. Now he was being called upon to save his sister.

But how?

What had he learned as a hunter?

Was this the one story he would never get to tell?

Confusion jarred his naïve thinking.

Questions came and went in fragments.

He struggled with the answers and ran and ran and ran.

AS HE TRIED to decide how to hunt down the Indian boy, Jake tightened his grip on his rifle as though it were his salvation and ran his other hand over his wet hair, his palm and fingers showing a translucent pink from the dye. He had forgotten his hat and trotted to the patch of snow where the raven had fallen. His black Mariners cap sat perched on top of the snow as though someone had placed it there for him as a gift, but the raven was gone. He put on his cap and studied the snow. There was no sign of the bird, no trail of blood. What the fuck was going on? He shook his head. There was no time for this. It was time to get to work.

He walked back to the cabin and peered through the window. His captives were as he had left them. He pulled open the door and leaned in. "You girls okay?" As he closed the door he heard Feather mutter, "Fuck you, you crazy bastard." He thought that her time would come.

He stood by the window, studying the Indian boy's boot prints, then followed them across patches of snow, noting that they grew further apart as the boy ran faster and faster. He smiled as the prints led him into the woods where the tracking was easier, snow still blanketing the ground in the shade of the trees. "You can run, but you can't hide," he called out. "You're dead meat, asshole."

He checked his rifle to make sure he was ready for his hunt, although he thought an Indian boy couldn't be much of a match for Jake Hornbeck, and followed the boy's boot prints. They seemed to track aimlessly through the trees as though the boy was confused on how best to escape. Jake was certain he was a frightened, panicked kid acting like a wild animal. It was only a matter of time.

Jake walked deeper into the forest, the rain rattling in the trees above him, and stopped to study the boy's tracks. They showed a shorter stride as though he had tired of running, changing direction randomly then following a straight line deep into the woods.

Jake thought the time was near and his heart began to race. He moved quietly, searching the woods with each step, and then he saw it, a small red speck close to the ground behind a thick blow-down. He drew a deep breath and let it out. The little son of a bitch had run out of gas.

He took another long, slow breath, tried to steady himself, and raised the rifle, carefully rotating the magnification knob on the sight as he had many times before in anticipation of a moment such as this. At the sight's full magnification he could clearly make out the red and white pattern of the boy's bandana, although he couldn't tell through the blow-down if the boy was facing him or facing away. He lowered the sharp black crosshairs beneath the bandana, trying to get a clearer picture of the boy's head but knew the heavy magnum bullet would plow through the brush and do its lethal job whether his adversary was hidden in the cover or out in the open. He steadied the crosshairs and squeezed the trigger. The rifle recoiled hard against his shoulder, its muzzle blast quickly swallowed by the woods.

Jake stood still for a moment as though he could not believe what had just happened. His back and chest burned with pain. He dropped his rifle and reached over his shoulders with both hands and flailed at his back, then tried forcing his hands upward, pawing and grabbing for the shaft of the small arrow that protruded between his shoulder blades. He coughed, and blood dripped from his mouth. He dropped to his knees, his heavily muscled arms still straining to reach the arrow, its shaft inches from his grasp. He tried to clear his head and figure out what to do next, but his world was slipping in and out of focus. He fell forward on his hands, still reaching in vain for the arrow with one hand and then the other.

He was tiring quickly and rested on all fours, trying to call back his discipline and his superhuman strength, all the while finding it harder and harder to concentrate. Out of the corner of his eye he saw the Indian boy steal through the woods, untie the red and white bandana from the brush he had wrapped it around, and re-knot it at the back of his head.

For an instant, the boy's face sharpened in detail. His eyes were wide and dark and seemed to Jake to look through him, and then the boy's eyes and all else melted into a blur again. Jake blinked to see more clearly. When he refocused, the Indian boy was standing over him, one booted foot covering the rifle, a hand on the handle of his bowie knife.

"Look at me, stranger," the boy said. "Why did you come here?"

Jake coughed again, his spittle a frothy, bright pink. He was determined not to give in and summoned all his strength to look at the Indian boy, but he was nowhere to be seen.

23

CARRIE JERKED HER HEAD from the pillow. "Oh my God, he's shot your brother!"

Feather's reply was cool and measured. "Maybe. Maybe not. At times he becomes one with the forest."

Carrie struggled to free herself, the nylon cord burning her wrists and holding her tightly in place as she twisted her hands one way and then the other. "That son of a bitch!" she sobbed. "What if he did kill him? What do we do then? He's going to kill us, too. I know he will, Feather. Please, think of something. For God's sake, think of something."

"Think of something?" Feather said. "Here's what I think: we're in deep scat unless my brother fooled your friend."

"He's not my friend!" Carrie cried.

Both were hushed by a shadow passing across the floor and the cabin door opening. Carrie gasped, "Please God, no!"

Storyteller stood in the doorway, gripping his bow.

"Sweet Jesus!" Carrie said.

"You can say that again," Feather said.

The boy glanced at Carrie's naked white body spread-eagled across the bed and then looked down at his sister. His dark eyes were filled with tears. He bit his lip and shook his head. "He won't cause you any more trouble," he whispered. His hands shook as he drew the large bowie from its scabbard and cut the cord from Feather's ankles and wrists.

When he was finished, Feather sat back on her haunches and massaged her wrists and looked up at him. "You okay?"

"I guess," he said.

Feather stood and opened her arms and pulled him to her.

For a moment the boy held his sister close and then stepped back, turned the bowie's handle toward her and offered her the knife. He nodded toward Carrie but refused to look at her. "You do her."

"You've never come across anything like that in the woods, now have you?" Feather said.

Again he pushed the knife's handle toward his sister and whispered, "Don't be a jerk."

When Feather had cut her free, Carrie sat and pulled her knees to her chest and reached to embrace her friend. Neither woman spoke until Feather looked over her shoulder at her brother. "What happened to the redhead?"

Storyteller stepped toward the open door and looked out at the gray day. The cabin was quiet except for the sound of the rain pounding on the roof.

"Well?" Feather said.

Storyteller glanced back at her. His dark eyes were bright with tears. "I shot him."

"With the rifle?" Feather asked.

He shook his head and looked back out the door. "With the bow."

Feather set the knife on the table and wrapped her arms around the boy from behind. She laid her cheek against his hair. "Don't worry little brother. You did the right thing. You know that, don't you?" The boy didn't answer. Feather rocked him in her arms. "It's all right," she whispered. "It's all right." She let another moment pass until she felt the boy's body begin to relax. "You've grown. You're as tall as I am," she said and kissed his cheek.

Storyteller folded his arms over his sister's. "It's always just been birds and rabbits and deer."

"I know," Feather said. "I know." She turned him to her and took his hands in hers. "I'm sorry, but it was him or us. He was going to rape Carrie, and maybe me, and kill us when he was through."

"You're sure?" the boy asked.

"No question about it. He had no choice, and you didn't either."

Storyteller nodded and reached a copper-colored hand to his face to hide his tears.

"God damn that bastard," Feather said. "Listen, little brother, please, listen. You saved our lives. Believe me, you did the only thing you could have. You *must* understand." She shook him by the shoulders and gave him a penetrating look. "Do you?"

The boy looked at the floor. "I guess."

Feather squeezed his shoulders hard. "No guessing. Okay?"

Storyteller looked up. "Okay."

Carrie stood to dress and again the boy turned toward the door. When she had finished dressing she walked to him and put out her hand. "I've heard a lot about you, and it's all true. Bart thought you were very special."

"I saw his resting place." He looked down and drew the toe of his boot in a short line across the floor. "How did he...?"

"His leg got mangled by a bear trap and he bled or froze to death," Carrie said.

"He was my friend," Storyteller said.

"And mine," Carrie said.

For the first time, Storyteller looked directly at her. "Who is that redheaded man?"

"A guy who wanted to get even with me and with Bart for taking me from him. He was crazy enough to want to kill us for that, so your sister was right: you did the right thing; it was either him or us." She paused. "What do we do with him now?"

"We'll bury him and hide any sign he's ever been here," Feather said. "I doubt he told whoever flew him here that he planned on killing us. So not to worry; people disappear out here all the time." She looked at Storyteller. "It's over. Okay?" She drew a deep breath. "Now, how about some breakfast?"

He said he hadn't eaten much except a couple of ducks and some jerky since crossing the Chitina.

While Carrie warmed two cans of beef stew, Feather brought the rifles in from the rain and wiped them dry and loaded each, setting one behind the door and resting the other on the nails above the stove. The rain stopped as suddenly as it had begun and she curled a finger at her brother. "Before we eat, I want to show you something special."

She led Storyteller across the damp grass to the foot of the totem. "Look," she said, running a finger across the lower figures. "There's McFee and Carrie, and their husky and her—" She was interrupted by a choking sound.

Jake was leaning against the outhouse, his pale gray face highlighted by his bright red hair and the blood that ran from the corners of his mouth. He struggled to raise the rifle and staggered a step toward them.

Feather looked at her brother. "I thought—"

"So did I," the boy said.

High above them, the raven cawed loudly as he glided toward the totem.

From inside the cabin Carrie smiled at the bird's calling and peered out the door to greet him. She was startled by the sight of Jake as he laid his cheek along the comb of his weapon and pointed it at Storyteller. Bloody spittle bubbled from his mouth as he muttered, "No one fucks with Jake Hornbeck."

Carrie grabbed the rifle from above the stove, levered a round into its chamber and stepped into the doorway. She pulled the rifle tight against her shoulder. Her heart beat quietly. Her vision was clear. Her breathing was easy. She knew what she must do: cock, aim and…squeeze.

Jake fell forward, his rifle discharging before his fall jammed the weapon's muzzle in the soft ground at his feet. For a second his body teetered on the spongy recoil pad and then he fell face down in the mud, the shaft of the small arrow still protruding from between his shoulder blades.

Carrie stared at what she had done, at what she thought she could never do.

The raven ceased to caw and settled quietly on the totem, and the camp was silent. Carrie levered another round into the rifle's chamber and watched to see if Jake showed any more signs of life and the magnitude of what she'd done overwhelmed her. Oh my God, she thought. She'd killed a man. This couldn't be her. She'd be wanted by the police. Hunted by them the way she was by him. What had she done? Where could she go?

She placed the rifle back on its nails and sat at the foot of the bed and covered her face with her hands. "I'm a murderer," she said aloud. "This has gone too far. Way too far. It was supposed to be about Bart and me and not all of this. I can't believe it."

Her sobs filled the cabin and she didn't hear Feather join her, but her touch was familiar as she laid her hand on her shoulder. "It's over, Carrie," she said and gently stroked her blonde curls. "There's nothing more to worry about."

Carrie looked up at her and rubbed her tears from her cheeks. "But I killed him, Feather. I'm a murderer. Now the police will be after *me*."

Feather patted her shoulder. She was smiling and Carrie thought it was a strange thing for her friend to do.

"I wouldn't worry, sister," Feather said. "You missed."

"But—"

"He fell just as you shot."

"Are you sure? You're not just saying that to make me feel better?"

"I'm sure," Feather said, and Carrie sensed, and desperately hoped, that her friend was telling the truth. "There's not a mark on him."

A quiet cough came from the doorway. Feather and Carrie turned and looked at Storyteller, his face dark in the hazy midday light that shone from behind him. "She's telling the truth. The arrow killed him."

"Honest?" Carrie said.

"Honest injun," Feather said and wrapped her arms around Carrie. "Now you're free to have your child. Free to start a new life."

STORYTELLER WORKED his arrow from Jake's back and dragged his rain-soaked body over the wet snow, deep into the woods, where Feather and he dug a grave in a small clearing. They eased the body into the hole, and there they buried Jake Hornbeck with all his possessions except his identification as Johnny Archer, his bus tickets, and his thick roll of money. Once they filled the grave, Storyteller told his sister he would finish camouflaging the site and covering their tracks so no one would ever discover their secret.

Feather walked back to the cabin, counting Jake's money as she went. She found Carrie seated in the doorway, her head resting against the doorjamb, sound asleep. Feather slipped by her, opened the grate to the woodstove and watched as the last evidence that Jake Hornbeck or Johnny Archer ever existed burned to black ashes.

The clanking of Feather closing the grate startled Carrie. "Where'd you come from?"

"We're done," Feather said. "No one will ever know he was here." She handed Carrie the wad of bills. "There are twenty-seven hundred dollars here."

"Twenty-seven hundred?"

Feather nodded. "I thought you said his name was Jake something. The tag on his pack said Johnny Archer."

Carrie stood and stuffed the money in the pocket of her fleece. "I guess that was his little game; that and dying his hair." She paused. "He really did come out here to kill Bart and me, didn't he?"

"Absolutely," Feather said, "after he raped you a bunch of times, most probably in front of Bart."

"That would have killed him," Carrie said and took Feather by the hand. "You want to pay him one last call? I need him right now."

"You go," Feather said. "Tell him all that's happened. I think it's important it's just the two of you, so you can…"

"Can what?"

"Say good-bye."

Carrie wrapped her long arms around the smaller woman and pulled her to her. "I guess the time is near."

24

THE SOUND of an airplane directly overhead drew Carrie, Feather and Storyteller from the cabin. They watched as a Super Cub flew in figure eights above the tree line, its blue and gold fuselage glinting in the bright sun as it worked its way closer to the cabin, circled above them and turned toward meadows in the distance.

"What's he doing?" Carrie asked.

"Looking for someone," Feather said. "Most probably someone with red hair."

"Oh, Jesus," Carrie said. "Could he know already?"

"No," Feather said, "so don't you tell anyone."

The plane turned and flew directly at them, its engine's growling growing louder and louder. A quarter of a mile away it turned once more and touched down and rolled to a stop. As the propeller coughed to a halt, a heavy-set man with a shock of white hair climbed down from the plane and ambled toward them. He waved and Carrie waved back. "It's Whitey," she said, and for some reason found herself smiling.

When Whitey was close to them, he pulled off his dark glasses and nodded. "Well, I'll be damned! Feather. Good to see you."

"And you, Whitey," she said.

He put out his hand to Storyteller. "Hey, son, how've you been?"

The boy shook his hand and told him that he'd been good.

Whitey lit a cigarette and looked at Carrie. "Well, Miss Ritter, how'd you enjoy the Riviera?" He paused. "Say, where's McFee?"

Feather and Storyteller looked at Carrie. She looked down at her feet. "He's...he's no longer with us. His leg got mangled in a bear trap and he never made it home."

"McFee's dead? Good Lord," Whitey said, pushing smoke through his nose. "Damn, I'm sorry." He shook his head. "I thought he could survive anything."

For a moment no one spoke. "Damn," Whitey said again. "One of Lola's traps, no doubt. Son of a bitch." He patted Carrie's sleeve. "It must have been rough for you. I'm sorry. Very...very damn sorry." He shook his head and muttered "sad news" and looked about the homestead and then at Feather. "I hate to change the subject but I'm looking for a guy I dropped off near here a week ago. He wanted to be picked up today but I can't locate him or his campsite anywhere."

"A guy?" Feather said.

"Yeah," he answered. "A prickly bastard with bright red hair. Said his name was Johnny Archer, but I think he was bullshitting me."

Feather shook her head. "Haven't seen anybody out here except these two and a bunch of caribou."

"Huh?" Whitey said. "Really?" He sighed. "Okay, I'll file a report when I get back to McCarthy on McFee and on this

Archer character. Maybe the rangers can find him. I didn't think he'd make it; he was just another city boy in over his head." He dropped his cigarette and tamped it into the wet ground. "Well, I'd better get going." He smiled. "Nice to see you all. Anything I can do for any of you back at civilization?"

Carrie looked at Feather and then at Whitey. "Can you fly that little plane to Anchorage?"

"Do it all the time."

"How much do you charge?" she asked.

"Four hundred, one way." He winked at Storyteller. "Cash on the barrelhead."

Carrie looked at Feather again. She felt the tears beginning to well, felt her knees begin to weaken. "Would you take me?"

Feather turned away.

"Yes, ma'am. Just name the day."

Carrie's heart began to race. "How about today?"

"Shit," Feather whispered.

"I'm sorry," Carrie said, "but it had to happen sometime."

"You're right," Feather said. "It's just so…so sudden, but you're right."

"Well, sir?" Carrie said.

"I can get you to Anchorage today if you'd like, but we can't dawdle."

Carrie laughed.

"What's funny?" Whitey asked.

"You sound like my mother; you and your 'dawdling.'" When she spoke she smiled at the thought of seeing her mother again, and Hannah, too, and telling them that she was expecting and describing all that she had witnessed in Alaska, or at least almost all. "How long's dawdling?" she asked.

Whitey looked at his watch. "You've got half an hour, but not a minute more. We need all the daylight we can get."

Carrie pulled Jake's roll of bills from her fleece and began to peel off the fare to Anchorage. Whitey whistled through his teeth at the sight of the money and cocked his head. He directed his question to Feather. "You sure you haven't seen this Johnny Archer character?"

"Positive," Carrie answered. She took five hundred dollars from the roll and handed it to the pilot. "The little extra's for a smooth flight. I'm pregnant."

Whitey whistled again. "I got a feeling that's not the only secret you're keeping, but you'll have a smooth flight. Feather can tell you, I'm a man of my word." He paused and laid his hand gently on Carrie's arm. "Did McFee know?"

Carrie felt tears begin to come again and rather than trying to speak, simply shook her head.

"Too bad. I knew him pretty well, and he'd have liked the idea of being a father," Whitey said. "Would have liked that a lot."

IN TWENTY MINUTES Carrie emerged from the cabin dragging her bulging duffle, her cell phone tucked in the breast pocket of Bart's black-and-white-checked shirt.

"I'll take that," Whitey said, reaching for the heavy bag. "In your condition you shouldn't be doing any heavy lifting." He nodded good-bye to Feather and turned to her brother and took his hand. "So long, Storyteller."

Feather shook her head. "From now on he's Littlelataw. He's no longer a boy; no longer just a storyteller."

"Roger that," Whitey said and smiled at Littlelataw, then shouldered Carrie's duffle, fumbled for another cigarette in his shirt pocket, and headed toward the meadow.

Carrie turned and studied the campsite, wondering if this was the last time she'd ever see it. The raven sat atop the totem and looked down at her. She smiled. "Well, my friend, our whole story told in a wooden pole. Well, almost our whole story."

She turned to Feather and started to say something but Feather interrupted her. "No long good-byes, and don't say you'll write or call, because you'll never reach me. If you want to find me, you'll have to come back out here. Same with Littlelataw. So let's just leave it at this: you've found friendship in the wilderness forever."

Carrie bit her lip.

"And don't worry about the cabin," Feather said. "You're leaving it better than you found it, which is all we ever ask."

Carrie took Feather in her arms and pressed her cheek hard against hers. "The cabin's yours, but I'll be back."

"With your child?" Feather said.

"Absolutely. Other than my Mom, you're the only family my baby will have." She looked into Feather's large brown eyes. "Bart was right. You are the best friend a person could ever have." The women embraced again, their tears mixing with each other's. Finally, Carrie stepped back and put out her hand to Littlelataw.

"Come on, Carrie, give him a kiss good-bye. It'll make his day," Feather said.

"Don't be a jerk," her brother said.

Carrie smiled and gently kissed the boy, her lips soft against his. "That's for saving my life, and for being such a fine young man. Please, take good care of your sister. She's my sister now, too."

Littlelataw nodded and stood in stunned silence.

Carrie squeezed his hand and gave Feather one last hurried hug before she skipped across the small creek that ran freely for the first time since she'd been in camp and jogged through the meadow toward Whitey and his shiny little blue and gold airplane.

"ALL SET?" Whitey asked.

Carrie sniffled and ran a finger under her nose. "I guess." She wiped away her tears and forced a smile.

"Okay, in you get." He took her hand and lifted her by her elbow to help her into the plane. "It's rough saying goodbye to friends, huh?"

Carrie mumbled, "It sure is," as she crawled into the cramped back seat.

Once settled at the controls, Whitey latched the door and looked at her over his shoulder. "Seat belt fastened? Headset on?"

Carrie said "yes" to both in a low voice.

"Okay. We're good to go."

She reached a hand for his shoulder to ask him to wait a moment, but changed her mind.

As though he'd sensed what she was thinking, he asked again, "All set?"

She paused and then whispered through her headset, "All set."

Whitey taxied to the edge of the meadow, turned the plane and sped it along the open space where Bart and she had spent so many cold, clear days and bright nights snowshoeing with Lola. He raised the nose gently, climbing over the trees to the west of the camp, banked the plane hard to the right and flew toward the cabin. Beneath them, Carrie could see Feather and Littlelataw standing by the totem, waving. She waved back and wondered if they could see her. Whitey tipped the plane's wings to the right and then to the left, saluting those on the ground before turning again and heading west.

Carrie looked from window to window, hoping for one more glimpse of Feather and her brother; perhaps even for a look at Bart's resting place, but all that was behind her and out of sight. She fell back into her seat and folded her hands in her lap when Whitey said, "We've got company."

To their left the raven flew above them, his eye closest to the plane a milky white. He tipped his large ebony wings, mocking his blue and gold cousin's salute, then soared away, dropping lower and lower, his shiny black form growing smaller and smaller, until he disappeared above the tundra. Carrie spread her hand against the window as though she were in some way protecting the bird and smiled. Well good-bye to you, too, she thought, and thanked him for looking after her.

"If you don't mind me asking," Whitey's voice crackled through her headset, "what happened back there? Was there a problem?"

"Just some unfinished business, that's all," Carrie said.

"Anything I should know? I can do? McFee was a regular guy and Feather and the boy are good people, too."

Carrie reached into the pocket of her fleece, pulled out the roll of bills, counted off a thousand dollars for herself and reached over the pilot's shoulder and handed the remainder to him. "Can you keep a secret?"

Whitey took the money and stuffed it in his shirt pocket. "That's part of my charm."

"Good," she said, her hand resting on his shoulder. "Nothing happened back there. Absolutely nothing."

"Doesn't surprise me," Whitey said. "Nothing much ever does."

Through her headset Carrie heard him laugh and then heard him say, "Look." He tapped the window and banked the plane sharply to the right. "A pack of wolves."

She straightened in her seat and searched the green meadow below her, now dotted yellow with dandelions. "Fly lower, please, Whitey. I'd like a closer look."

"You got it." He put the plane in a gentle dive, leveled out and then circled above the wolves.

From the low altitude Carrie could easily identify the male by his size and black and buff coloring. As the plane's shadow passed over them, one of the animals looked up, her pale blue eyes caught for a moment in the sunlight. "Jesus, it's Lola!"

"Pardon?" Whitey said.

Carrie ignored him, but still speaking through her headset said, "And one, two, three, four…five, six…seven. They're all there. Thelma and Louise and the basketball team. Thank God. Can you wave your wings to them?"

"Okay, but then we've got to head west."

As the plane circled low above the pack, Carrie waved from the window, smiling through her tears and Daredevil, Lola and their pups stretched their muzzles upward and opened their mouths. The drone of the Super Cub's engine drowned out their sounds but Carrie could imagine their howling chorus and thought of the lines from Walt

Whitman's *Song of Myself* that she'd loved so, the poem she'd read to Bart on Christmas night after the pups were born: *I think I could turn and live with animals, they are so placid and self-contain'd, I stand and look at them long and long. They do not sweat and whine about their condition, They do not lie awake in the dark and weep for their sins* ...

The wolves grew more distant as the plane began to climb to altitude and head toward Anchorage, toward home. Carrie waved one last wave and smiled. "Be well, Lola, you naughty, naughty girl!"

"Pardon?" Whitey said again.

"Nothing, Whitey," Carrie said. "Nothing. Nothing at all."

Acknowledgments

Many thanks to veteran book and magazine editor Betty Sargent for her enthusiastic and unfailing support. Also, thanks to Anne Dubuisson Anderson, Chris Noel, Hugh Cook and Emily Heckman for their valuable criticism, and thanks to the *Writing Aloud* program of The InterAct Theatre in Philadelphia for performing "Daredevil" in a reading taken from *Thirty Below's* early chapters.

About the Author

HARRY GROOME's short stories, poems and articles have appeared in dozens of magazines and anthologies and have won several awards. He's the author of the novel *Wing Walking* and the Stieg Larsson spoof *The Girl Who Fished with a Worm*. A graduate of the University of Pennsylvania, Harry also holds an MFA in writing from the Vermont College of Fine Arts. He and his wife, Lyn, and his two dogs split their time between Villanova, PA and the Adirondack Mountains in NY.

Visit Harry's website at www.harrygroome.com